<u>RIDES</u>

A Novel

by

Tim Hoopingarner

D1005217

Copyright © 2013 Tim Hoopingarner

All Rights Reserved

To my Fano:

Small groups and large, near and far.

I am connected to you now.

Table of Contents

Preface

It took me a long time to get started on this trip... a long time to get myself on my feet, and then to get the feet moving in a way necessary to cross the country without the guidance of others. Maybe nine months or so. Nine long months, with the idea starting as a small seed one evening while tossing the ideas of the world around, with someone else who had heard the rumors. We had talked about the rumors of "The West," the "Big West," with the mountains and the sky, and the remarkable abilities of those who journeyed there, free of the constraints of home, Ohio.

Our bible was *On the Road* by Jack Kerouak, and every drinking buddy chattered away about how they'd find their way "Out West" to evolve into wise monks of the road. I chattered along with them, the romantic vision digging deeper and deeper into my gut as we rolled ideas around. I dreamed I was Neil, I dreamed I was Jack, I dreamed I was someone who never existed.

The goal, at least when I started, was to become a man... and that meant getting to the West Coast, to bathe my feet in the Pacific Ocean, to walk the "Golden Road" of Routes 1 and 101. I had the vague notion that I would somehow *know* how to live my life if I attained these goals, as if the experience would impart to me the gift of truth, the gift of knowing how to live life. Of course, none of that ever came to pass, and when I finally did arrive on the coast, I found myself needing to figure out what to do with myself from there... and on it went like that.

Nine rather long months, full at first of infrequent thoughts, progressing to a state of mind which left me preoccupied with the idea of traveling west, under my own power, in my own command. It was a blessing to at last get started.

The gestation was a long one, until, at last, in a phone call to Michael, who was in Michigan at the time, the thoughts formed into reality. Then, pregnant with emotion and ideals, I rushed headlong into preparations for "The Road," gathering quickly the tools I would need to crawl across the huge expanse of our rich and foreboding nation.

Foreword

This book was written in two different time frames. Part One, the beginning part of the journey, was written from the point of view of Edwin "Fast Eddie" Wanderhaven when he was a young man in his late teens and early twenties. His tone reflects the view of a youngster out in the world for the first time.

Parts Two and Three, encompassing the middle and end of the journey, were written from recorded interviews when Eddie was in his sixties. The latter parts are in essence transcriptions of Mr. Wanderhaven's spoken words.

There are three distinct parts to the story. Like a human lifecycle, it represents youth, middle age, and old age. In Part One, the chapters written from interviews are so noted and are observations by Eddie when he was an older man.

Prologue

"Well, there's one thing I have to tell you before we get started: things really *were* kinda different back then. I know it's not *that* long ago, but it really was kinda different. For one thing, the freight haulers didn't have air conditioning... I mean, forget all the fancy bunks and all that, hell, they didn't have air. So, when you caught a ride with a hauler going from say Flag to Phoenix, you had to be ready to take a beating, not just the heat itself, mind you... but the way that hot hair banged in the window, it felt like a beating!

"My journey includes the years of transition in our country, from the old federal two-lane roads that connected our major cities to the Interstate freeway system that now nets the maps. The freeways are a lot better for a hitchhiker, as people are sure to be going a number of miles, whereas the old two-lane roads would often provide for only a mile or two at a time (nice people trying to help, even if only a little bit, but frustrating to someone trying to cover miles).

"You just don't see people on the side of the road now the way you used to see 'em. Man, I've been on exit ramps where there'd be twenty, maybe twenty-five people waiting for a ride... hell, I don't ever see more'n one *ever*, and even that's pretty rare these days. And let me tell you, when you're in a crowd like that, you gotta use your head to figure out how you're gonna get down the road... you can't just hope that a driver is gonna pluck you out of a crowd (although even that happened to me once, stoned to the bone, on a turnpike ramp in Ohio)... you gotta either make yourself different from the

4

crowd or find another way around it: walk to the next exit, maybe look for a freight train nearby, whatever.

"I just think people have more money these days. I mean, everyone still complains about the economy, loss of jobs, all that, but you don't see people hitchhiking the way we did when we were so broke. Hell, my mom had me take my little brother to the *dentist* by hitchhiking... he wasn't more than eleven years old. They'd cry 'child abuse' if they saw that now!

"Food was another thing. First of all, we didn't have any money... I mean, that's why we were hitchhiking, right? Sometimes a fella would go two days without a bite, and when he did eat, it'd be bread or maybe a head of lettuce from the grocery store. I still remember that Korea veteran who had a plate in his head... he asked when was the last time I ate, and when I couldn't answer his question, *he* felt pity for *me*! And then he took me inside and we ate a big meal. He just asked me to pass it on, and years later I did, to a skinny, hungry hitcher down in Gallup. Felt good to repay the favor.

"We didn't have the luxury of bathing all that often, either, we or the truckers. So, if you were a little ripe from the road, the haulers understood that... maybe *that's* why the windows were open all the time!

"I saw on TV the other day that there are people who can remember just about every day of their lives. Although I do admire them, I'm not even sure I *want* that! So, what I share with you isn't the exact truth... I'm sure Mikey would disagree with me on many points. The thing is, as we travel through life, time becomes inexact and distorted. Places lose focus and seem to move around. So, I'll share the best I can, but you have to remember, it was a long time ago, and the story of my journey is just that: *my* story of my journey.

"But the other thing I want to say is more personal. I can see it now, but I could never see it back then. I just didn't have any feelings back then. I mean, I hardly ever ate sometimes, and like I said, bathing was a rare treat. Clothes would wear out, but you can always go to a church rummage sale and replenish your rags for under a dollar… at least you could back then. But I mean personally, coming out of my family's home, I just didn't feel *connected* to people. I didn't write home or even call much, so they didn't know where I was. I actually really liked being on the road, because the human interactions were just the way I liked them: short, purposeful, and with a defined end. Hitchhiking fit me perfectly… it's what I called 'hit and run.' Just like at a party, where I'd talk to someone for a few minutes then duck away, drink my beer, and then have another real short conversation. Most folks found me really convivial (if that's the right word), but the truth was I couldn't stand to get close to anyone. Not at all. I pity the girlfriends I had back then… I was like Houdini the escape artist! So, the rides I got started out just the way I wanted them to… I didn't speak unless the driver spoke. Sometimes with freight haulers, especially if they had a Citizens Band radio squawking constantly, we wouldn't say a word in fifty miles! I just felt unfit for other humans… I didn't feel worthy of closeness with anyone. It hurts me to say that, but it's the truth. Now, as the journey wore on, I learned more and more about liking people and about being able to stay with them for a conversation, but it was a long and difficult road to that spot. I'm very grateful for the full revolution of the journey, of the wheel going all the way around, because my life is good now, and I can be with people without squirming out of my hide... I can connect with people, and I actually have love in my life now.

"Imagine that!"

Hunger

We were always hungry. Physically and otherwise.

On this day I wore a headband of cloud on my forehead, but Michael only smiled.

"Let me show you a trick," he said.

Holding his left forearm on the horizontal in front of his abdomen, he rolled his wrist over, so the heel of his hand faced out. Placing his right hand on the heel of the left, he firmly pushed that big first knuckle up under his ribs on the left side of his body. "See?"

I was shocked that I actually burped. Then I noticed the pangs subside... "It really works!" I whispered in awe.

I've used that trick a lot of times.

<u>Part One</u>

Chapter One

Genesis

"I guess if I went all the way back to the beginning, it would have to be from a story my mother told... well, more than one, really. But the one about me breaking up the playpens in which I was confined never really sat well with me, so I'm gonna leave that out. The one I mean is where she was pushing me in a stroller... in those days, it was more proper for strangers to stop and say "such a beautiful baby" and that sort of thing than it is now, and so a young mother could go out walking with a little finery on and be proud of wheeling her baby around. She told me much later that I never just sat back in the stroller but was always erect, feet planted, head forward, and my arm out in front, a pudgy finger always at the prow. I gabbled away, she said, as if to say: 'Look at that!' and 'Now that!' and on and on, ever surprised by the world's bright colors, always eager for the next sight.

"That image is the one that sticks with me, and it's not even my image!

"Mother is long dead now, but still my mind gabbles, my spine straining forward: 'Look! Look at that!' "

Chapter Two

King of the Road

I began the journey the third week in March. Much too early for comfort, something I realized only too late, after I had begun my fateful journey. I started in fairly conventional fashion, getting a long ride in mother's vehicle down to the turnpike. I checked and re-checked the map before I got out and bid goodbye. The trip was a bit unconventional due to my mode of travel. I was not entirely happy with the process of slipping out of mother's warm carriage into the cool after-rain of the day, but I set a grim smile and, despite a tear or two, prepared to hit "The Road," at last.

We experienced a bit of awkwardness in my departure, me opening and then closing the door repeatedly in saying goodbye to her (and to my past way of being). She seemed in physical pain. Finally, however, with a surge, I moved out of the tight confines, my lungs expanding with the cool air of freedom, and grabbed my small pack from the backseat. With a grunt, bordering on a cry, I slammed the door, and she pushed away to watch me depart.

So began my journey toward manhood, toward the great unknown West and the Pacific Ocean.

Resolutely, I flagged at the autos going by, infantile in my motions. I was not really prepared for this, and at first I was stiff and uncomfortable trying to catch a ride. Finally, I scored a kind, elderly doctor heading west. Not too far west, but a start, and I hopped into his car.

We stopped at the toll booth, and the uniformed matron precisely checked the time, withdrew a slip, and handed it to the good doctor. I suddenly felt myself moving, slipping into a new world, and I was filled with apprehension and fear.

As the ride swept me down the entry-ramp, I felt myself turning. I squirmed uncomfortably in the car and felt a pounding in my head. I strained to turn and look back again at the woman, but suddenly I felt myself being crowned by forces beyond my control. I felt crowned by a destiny which I could not see, on a journey that I could not understand. I was crowned, and then in an instant, I, Edward T. Wanderhaven, was born a "King of the Road." The realization brought me to tears, and the kindly doctor patted me softly and firmly between my shoulder blades, reassuring me that all would be well, despite my involuntary spasms and sobs. "All will be well. All will be well," he muttered again.

Chapter Three
Getting Started

It's not as easy as it may sound: getting started, that is. There is certainly the excitement, and the nervousness, and all that, but what is really happening is a deep personal shift, a focus out of the ordinary, a deep breath before plunging into chilly water.

It's clean, sort of, too. It has all the stuff of that one and only fistfight in Cleveland, the excitement of getting ready, the knowing that it's going to feel so good and so horrible, so justified and so unfair, all these at the same time. And of course the final decision to plunge in, probably after it's too late anyhow. It has all that stuff, but probably is a lot cleaner in a lot of ways. No, not probably: *is* cleaner in a lot of ways.

There is all of that *fake* planning shit. All of the ideas, putting things in and then taking them back out right away. A lot of misconceptions about what's around the bend and a lot of wondering what the hell's going to happen.

But finally, thank God, there is the *real* planning shit, about an hour before you're ready to go, and then suddenly you know what it's going to be like and just settle down and get ready for that.

Well, it is a lot harder than it sounds, really.

It's sort of like that idiot fight down in Cleveland. There was a lot of excitement about that, too. I remember that kid only in a blur now, although I had probably seen him around for several weeks. There was all that fake buildup shit for hours before, with him badmouthing and then taking back, real mean and then real friendly. And there were the variables that always weigh in: too much alcohol, loud music, too many people... these are really the things that make it dirty and blurry. It should have been clean emotion, getting started. But at any rate, after all the fake shit, and all the time, and all the alcohol, there came that crystal clear moment of knowing what it was going to be like: with all the dreadful, ugly feelings, and joyful, sick feelings of brutal assertion. And there was that last moment, when I already knew that it was too late, when I took the cold plunge, when the thinking was over...

Well, getting started is a lot like that, only with a cleaner slate and an exploded sense of time. Of course, one already knows that there is much more to be enjoyed, a longer frame of reference for time, and that the times are to be clean in their brutality: honest as nature and as tempered as hardest steel. Not like that fight, which was short, and nasty, and smeared into a blur. Like the whole plan: nature, taken as a whole, with rules plain to those who wish to read. That's what the expectations are like, when they are real, for in that short time before departure, the expectations match the events in their feelings.

Chapter Four

Changing Gears

The good doctor took me only a little ways west, and then he needed to turn off and continue on local roads. I was reluctant to let go of such a nice beginning, so I stayed with him into the farmland, where I eventually found myself on a lonely two-lane.

It was a long wait for the next ride: a beat-up green pickup with rounded fenders and cab, spider-web back window, and if I'm not mistaken, a wooden floor in the bed.

Of course, there were always times when I could resent the entire hitchhiking situation. It was ludicrous, in fact, that I should be living my life as if there were no other means of relating to others than the simplistic and smiling "I'm sorrys" which would constantly roll off my lips. I could see the present gentleman was in no shape or mood to accept that kind of crap from a fresh-faced kid like me in the middle of the fucking farmlands. Of course, he was drunk. I knew that the minute he eyed me over before pulling off the road for me to run and hop in. It was obvious that the old truck was accustomed to that sort of post-work behavior, as the bed was full of the detritus of innumerable stops at the local hideout, maybe Bob's Café.

Of course, the ride could have gotten off to a better start, with me perhaps looking a little less bright, and perhaps a little less eager than I must have appeared in the early part of this first trip. He was in the mood for the manly sort of ride, filled with silence and the gurgle of beer bottles tipped up. But of course I was *too* fucking bright and eager, and the driver felt a little nauseous at having picked up such a load. I'm sure of it.

15

Slowly, however, the long wide patches of northwestern Ohio rolled past our tiny pickup, and soon the silence of the land calmed my jumping muscles. I was no match for the driver's dirty, stern face and his bright, fearsome eyes. There was no question about his advantage: his tipped-back ball cap and the way he slammed through the ancient gears. I was in for an uncomfortable silence, although I learned that this helped me. The silence was exactly the way to face my escape from the homeland, to ready me for the nights alone in the outer world, beyond my meager understanding of our country and the cosmos.

Actually, he was probably a pretty nice guy in his evenings off: couple of kids, a fair income from his filthy but skillful profession, and a home which he knew how to maintain. The sort of fella that keeps the heartland of America pumping, keeping the soy beans, the sugar beets, and the corn flowing to the businessmen who look down on farmers. A pretty nice guy, no doubt. These thoughts passed through my head as I stared out the passenger's window, listening to the loud radio twang and hitting sporadically on my Budweiser beer. Staring across the wide, boring, rich flatlands of the very breast of America and thinking of the intimidating man next to me. I was sure that he was probably a pretty nice guy, and I was trying hard not to get too uppity about the state of his personal hygiene and also trying hard not to breathe through my nose. But I was shifting gears with the man; I could feel it in my head, and in my hands, and in my jumpy legs. I knew that he was preparing me for the path, and the path would contain many more men who appreciated both loud twanging *and* human silence.

I was at last gaining calm with the black-and-blue figure next to me: his dark blue clothing and his piercing blue eyes. The man with the unshaven face and oil-stained hands.

I planned to hop out at a certain intersection, with the hope that the crossroad would be a little busier than this two-lane. That road would take me to a town near the *real* highway, the one out of the state, and I was eager to make the connection to that pulsing vein. In the droning heat, with me half-asleep, the man began to slow and pull over, and I began to panic: what's the problem? I thought. He, of course, knew where the intersection was and was letting me out... it took me a moment to collect myself and understand. Time to disembark. I was grateful, and I imagined that I had learned great lessons from the man. I turned, lifting my bag out of the bed of the pickup and, with my hand on the open door, began babbling away my goodbyes. He lifted a hand, slipped the clutch, and caused my door to slam shut as he sped across the crossroad (in a hurry to beat a line of traffic backed up behind a hog truck, which passed me with a powerful and vile wind). I heard the twenty-year-old gears winding up as the prophet gunned her across that road, and I understood that *I* was still in first gear, winding her too high and jumping the clutch too rough. But at least I was rolling. Finally, hurrying, I beat the lines of cars across the road.

From the guy in the pickup, I changed hands to an older farm wife who likened me to her son, who was stationed in South Carolina. I was surprised briefly at her stopping for me. But she was an open, strong, noble country lady and was certainly no threat to me, nor I to her. The ride was short and happy, with us two relating funny family stories and me trying to hide the beer on my breath. She was certainly knowledgeable but accepting, and we got on well until she dropped me at a crossroads just a few miles from the town of my destination. We parted with a wave.

My only armor for this adventure was the addresses of a few friends, but that was all. I was headed to one of the addresses now. The final miles into town were flat, nondescript, and uninteresting, in the manner that the Midwest now always strikes me. I finally flagged down a commuting student, who brought me into town with stories of his new job and his radio blaring. I lurched from the vehicle with my pack just a couple hundred yards from my destination, which was an address belonging to a drinking buddy of some repute.

I opened Teddie's unlocked door, after waiting several minutes, to find the place as empty as my belly. The apartment, of course, was in typical austere shambles, without a working light bulb. The refrigerator hummed along without a morsel, other than the usual greasy bottles of ketchup, relish, and mustard, a regular hot dog playground. I felt urgent over breaking my fifty-five-dollar bank, but my stomach overruled my money worries. Leaving a long explanative note, and trying to hide my bag in a back bedroom, I sprang out the front door, only to fall into the hands of a mob of drunken rowdies. The result would be as clear as nature's blueprint from that moment forward, for that night, these loud and obnoxious drunks were my pals, returning from an afternoon's watering.

The din, in the narrow walk between two apartment houses, left the only sober one feeling self-conscious. Loud whistles, continuous banter, and a long series of back-pounding followed.

I won't bore you with the details. It was the usual results when you pour beer into a hungry tummy. The night long, loud, and blurry, ending with a struggle to find my way to a bed, or in this case, a bit of cleared carpet. After a toxic sleep, I awoke bloodshot and bleary and once again starving. I rumbled with the popcorn dinner of the night before and, as I was strangely alone in the apartment, looked in vain once more for decent food. I gratefully showered, drying myself with the sweatshirt from my little bag. Leaving a little note for my missing-in-action host, I stumbled forth to meet the new day.

And so it goes: changing hosts, changing gears, up and down the scale. One moment of quiet and family and dignity; the next, drunken and obscene. But sooner or later, the gears always drop back to first. You can gear up 'til you're flying down the freeway with a thousand other travelers; but you always have to drop back to gear one, start *crawling* again, before you really start moving.

Chapter Five

In God We Trust

In the 1960s, we had a phenomenon known as "Jesus Freaks." I suppose these folks are always around, but they had a certain edge at that time: lots of conversations about talking with God (I often regaled others afterward with the "And what did God say back?" line) and being saved by angels, that sorta stuff.

Mostly these folks who gave me rides were gentle people who were trying their best to do the Lord's work, including a young woman in California (much later in my journey) who was so obviously nervous about picking up Mike and me, but must've felt it was her Godly duty... she immediately asked that we not harm her, to which we agreed... it wasn't a long ride, and we bid her well upon parting, but I always remembered how frightened she seemed of doing that kind deed... and I don't blame her.

Anyway, I got picked up by a group of three or four of these Jesus Freaks, and things started out all right... they shared their views with me, which was okay, and said where they were going, just down the road to an eatery, and all seemed well. I felt an aloof bemusement toward these folks, and as it was sprinkling rain, my attention seemed a small price to pay for warmth and progress down the road.

Things turned odd when we reached the restaurant.

Whenever I snagged a ride with someone who stopped to eat, it was always unclear about whether or not the driver was buying, and the situation was the same here. Lucky thing, I was smart enough to bring my little bag into the restaurant with me, as it otherwise woulda been locked in their car.

They weren't buying.

They were selling.

However, they suggested that they'd take me farther down the road if I just held on until they finished, so although I hadn't eaten of late, I tried to control my saliva and be pleasant while they ate. Thing was, they thought they held me captive, as we were now a mile or so off the highway, there was a gulley of an irrigation ditch between the restaurant and the byway, and, of course, it was raining.

The tone changed from one of pleasant inquiry and exchange to one of demanding to know if I was joining them in their religious views. I immediately felt a knot in my chest but tried to soldier on, preferring that to the wind and a long walk. The conversation took a decided twist when I asked a provocative question about their religious beliefs, something along the line of "If there is one God over all men, why would he be jealous?" or some such. The only response I got was a prayer hastily muttered by the leader of the group. At first I was confused, and there was an awkward silence, so I asked again, to be met by a louder refrain of the same, and I began to realize that the prayer had to do with lifting the evil out of *me*! I was a bit flabbergasted, you might imagine, as I, despite a variety of detours, have tried to live a somewhat righteous life. I began to speak again, perhaps a bit louder, but was drowned out by the loud incantations of our boss... I really do think that he thought he had me trapped or something. He now prayed very loud and *very* fast, something I wasn't used to, almost as if, if he didn't hurry up, the Lord might get bored and stop listening.

I hated to give up the ride and face the walk back to the drizzly two-lane, so I tried one last time: "Listen fellas, either answer

21

my question, or I'm..." I never did finish, as the hubbub drowned me out... the others had joined in by this time. I was shocked... certainly my ego was bruised, perhaps even more by the sense that disagreement should be simply drowned out. Even in such a tiny congregation!

Religious hubris is an obscenity, no matter what cloak, flag, or symbol it's shrouded in. That shit felt just like home.

I prefer the "God of Freedom."

I'd had enough, so I grabbed my bag and headed for the door, really grateful that I was fully self-contained and not trapped by having my bag locked in their car. Although the drainage ditch was deep, it was running only a foot or so in the bottom; I dropped down, crossed, and climbed back up without much trouble. Sure enough, I had a long walk to the highway, but it was worth it to get away from that narrow-mindedness. I kept looking over my shoulder to see if those fellas would overtake me, but they never did.

College towns are full of cheap eats, and I found another pancake house squatting on the fringe of the two-lane. I settled into my mantra, "Eat Everything," and kept asking for more coffee and butter and such, until the staff became uncomfortable with me. The waitress and I finally came to a mutual agreement that it was time to go. Though soggy and uncomfortable, I was warmed within by the coffee and pancakes and was eventually able to catch a ride headed west.

Chapter Six

Under a Bridge in the Rain

There's nothing quite like squatting under a concrete freeway bridge in a cold rain... especially in the Midwest. The sky is uninterrupted gray, and the rain makes of it an infinity. I moved up high under the bridge, as the wind was whipping rain into the middle part... I could feel the trucks above me rumbling in my gut, and the deep cold of the concrete seeped into my haunches. My balls chilled. I shivered.

Desultory.

Discouraged.

Damp.

I fretted about finances and the great length I had to travel. I had on the ridiculous bright-orange poncho that served as the ground cloth for my little tent... some of the moisture ran off, but none of the chill.

I began to feel my skin thicken. My edges drew in a fraction, making my borders just a bit more firm. The hardness and the cold pressed into me from all sides so that I shrank into a smaller, yet more substantive, firmer human. I felt a certain gravity in my low gut, below my navel.

I didn't welcome this, nor celebrate... only noticed what the world had for me.

There's nothing quite like squatting under a concrete freeway bridge in a cold rain. It helps redefine you. The problem is getting a ride from someone when you're dripping wet... not a lot of Midwesterners cotton to that kind of thing. After a while, you move back down to the roadside and finally someone will have pity on you, but they'll insist that you stand in the rain shaking the rain off of your coat before you get in, that sort of thing.

Especially when you're hungry, that cold and gray can really take you down to size. But I suppose everyone goes through that kind of hardening process in one way or another.

Chapter Seven

Mother

She would be shocked to hear it, but probably the main reason I took to life on the road is due to my poor mom. She's passed now, so I can say a thing or two without fearing that I'll hurt her or embarrass her. Embarrassment was a very big thing to Mother. If she felt *deeply* embarrassed, she might do anything. For instance, when I was ten years old, I played too rough with one of the girls from school, and her dad called my mom to complain. She had *my* dad wake me up late at night for a beating with the belt. I never did understand what the offense was, but I now believe it was that Mother was embarrassed, and that was the real sin.

Mom was a woman that walked on glass. All the time. She was deathly afraid of the Old Man, and she never could speak up for herself. But it went beyond that... she was a wraith... I could never quite get my arms around her. I never knew what she thought, or how she felt, or what the real truth in any given situation was. A lot different than the mother I finished my journey with. And she had the ability to really hurt me with her words... they'd strike like a snake, lightning quick, and deeply hurtful. Now, I've twice had real snakes try to bite me, and both times I was quick enough and scared enough to get out of the way... but I never could with Mom... she always hit her mark.

So although we would never have seen it, my own poor understanding of Mom was a solid part of why I hit the road. Despite my general numbness, the house was just too painful for me, and I felt safer out in the world.

Mom of course protested a bit as I packed my little bag, as any good mother would, but I think she knew as well as I that I needed to get out of the house. Besides, she had four younger ones to deal with, and it was a kind of pressure-relief for us all.

In the end, it was ironic that Mom took me to the highway in the family car. In a way, I kind of snuck out of the house, not saying goodbye to the rest of the family, as I just couldn't face an emotional goodbye, and besides, I was very eager. I had just a little money, and a rough idea of where I was heading, and a few friends' houses to visit along the way, and that was enough for then. Mother was sad about my departure, but she was the one who nudged me out of the nest.

Chapter Eight

Beast of Burden

It was probably because it was so damnable cold that the rig turned on its behemoth flashers and began to groan to the side of the entrance ramp. The horrid cold, and the fact that the ramp had enough of a grade to hide us from the attendants in the toll booths.

I was still in Ohio, still in a damp spring, and once again working my way onto the turnpike going west. He seemed to respond to my sign, and it was good that he was headed exactly there, or I might have been standing in the god-awful sleet for another couple of hours.

It was novelty, climbing the giant's side, clinging to a rail with one hand and unable to open the door, grinning foolishly at the driver. Recognizing my situation, he threw on the hissing parking brake, leaned over the wide console, and unlocked the door. His greased-back hair and toothy, straining grin were framed in the side window of the monster cab-over.

I clambered in, shivering with the cold, and dropped my sign on the high, wide dashboard. "Best set that on the floor, son," he hollered to me above the din of the racing engine. "They'll be on me in a second if they see that sign in the winda!" We rolled, roaring, to the toll gate and picked up a ticket without a word. I gradually relaxed in my seat and began to strip off my soaked poncho and sweatshirt.

This guy is a real truck driver, I smiled to myself. I beamed with the romantic thoughts of riding with a real jammer, light with the expectations of becoming a real wandering man with these grizzly characters as my pals.

I noticed that the seat was no great comfort to my soaking ass.

The driver was not really that grizzly, either. He was certainly a hard-pressed guy, and I admired him as he slammed through the gears with the roar and whistle of the diesel beneath us. Pushing and pulling through the gears, pausing to upshift the rear axle as we wound up the cloverleaf to the real highway. I was thrilled at the prospect of his distance and tried to imagine the thousands of miles he pounded out in this beast. I tried to imagine the different lands he'd seen and the way in which he would treat his monster rig in different climates.

"Where ya haulin?"

"Whaaat?"

"Where ya headed?"

"Over ta Elkhart!"

"Whatcha haulin?"

"Gotta loada insulation for a house trailer factory ovah there."

An Elkhart mobile home factory? My visions of desert sands were swept away with the rainy wind which now whipped against the flanks of the beast.

"How far is it?" My voice was already getting sore from the shouting.

"Whaaat?"

"How far is it?"

"Is what?"

The confusion and noise left me feeling hopeless of a meaningful conversation with my new pal. I decided, though he really was a salty-enough dog, to close it up quick.

"Elkhart!" I yelped.

"Oh. Another hunnerd miles or so."

Dismal hardly describes it. So my sign reading "WEST" hadn't gotten me to the West, but rather a mere hundred miles in that direction. I slumped a bit lower in the bony seat and imagined what it would be like to hop out in the midst of this downpour. The glory of the trip began to fade, and I wondered why I *had* to start in the spring. At that precise and palpable moment, I began to feel the roughness of the ride.

I thought I might best prepare myself by clamming up, analyzing this plight with my brain hiding below the roar, and swish, and deep growling hum of the rig in motion. It crossed my mind, for the first of several times before I attained the West Coast, that it might be best to turn back. That fifty bucks wasn't really enough to get across this wide continent, and this venture was a farce that no fool should embark upon.

However, no sooner had I slunk into this cavernous thought than the driver began an incessant shouting. He had, as I had once hoped and now loathed, picked me up for the company and wanted to shout a couple of stories, perhaps to stay awake and aware.

"Shit, a little rain and the whole damn freeway's nothin' but bad drivers!"

Mercifully, I was able to sustain him with a tentative nod and a smile.

"This rig'll put 'em to shame... if the damn bears'd let us run the way we want... hell, I could take the curves in this road better'nem four-wheelers will, and at twice the speed... hell, I ain't even got her in high gear yet!"

I glanced at the gearshift, and sure enough, despite our harrowing speed, it appeared that he had another higher gear at his command.

"You'd think these rigs'd be slow inna rain, but with a load on, I'm the safest vehicle on the road!" He shouted and shouted, turning to me at intervals for approval. I couldn't grasp the logic of what he was saying, but I nodded and nodded, smiling all the while.

"Shit, man, just look at the way that guy drives!"

I leaned forward in the seat to look back in the side mirror and saw a woman in a small foreign car struggling at the reins as we blew past her. Her small orange four-wheeler swerved in our after-mist, righted itself, and slowed to let our wind pass. I sat back in my seat and saw the driver's humor in the situation. I smiled, this time genuinely.

And so we rolled along, with the driver alternating between the scrambled squawking of his CB radio and his shouting out short stories and dirty jokes to me. Gradually, I fell into a half-sleep, with the slap of the windshield wipers and the deadening garble on the radio.

Suddenly, I felt the truck drop a gear, the new ratio winding down as the driver pump-braked the rig. I suddenly felt very sick. Without looking, I asked, "Is this it?" and started grabbing for my pack.

He smiled a big, toothy grin. "Naw, naw, just a piss call." He slammed and yanked at the gears as we slowed and, pumping the brakes through the rain, finally eased the big-shouldered rig into the rest-stop lot.

Leaving it running, we clambered down the sides of the beast, me with all fifty dollars in my pocket. My legs felt jelly-like, and I immediately noticed the ache in my back. He noticed me stretching, my arms akimbo on my low back, and snorted. "That seat's a little stiff, innit?" I was unsure what he meant but didn't smile. I asked him in my most serious truck-driver tone what the difference was.

"Well, hell, I got to have one of these hydraulic seats, or I'd be as sore as you." I now remembered the complex underpinnings of his seat and the ease with which he sat in the saddle. "Sort of a rough ride, huh?" He smiled, but an understanding one, and we strolled into the little plastic diner as new pals.

I was a little surprised by what my slightly beardy compadre shared as we sipped and mumbled over our coffee. I expected him to be hardcore, a concrete eater, a man of the hardened world.

He told me about his family.

"...and the little one's just started first grade..." I imagined his tiny daughter waking to the sound of his arriving late in the night.

"...and the boy's been liftin' weights to get ready for his first season." His son, perhaps a strong, awkward youth with but fleeting memories of his father, lifting weights to his absence, to the glory of manliness.

I saddened, let down a bit by the man's mortality, which was chafing against my colorful visions of the rough and loud truck-driver community. The rain beat on the window-wall next to us, and the jammers screamed by on the highway outside.

I sipped my coffee and grew more anxious to go as the clock let the time slip by. My driver, however, had the nonchalance of a tourist, pouring sugar in his coffee and toying with stories as we leaned on our elbows. "Never could stand the stuff, but I must drink a gallon a day." He stirred four spoons of sugar into a refreshed cup of thin mud. "I need the stuff to stay awake, you know?" I said I did know, as the coffee hit my nerves, setting my stomach to perspiring over the length of time we were spending in this unattractive pit stop.

"My wife used to pack me up a big jug of coffee, fulla sugar, and I'd drink that for the first day out. Got so's I couldn't keep the jug clean, though, and the trick of the thing is to get outta the cab once in a while, let my eyes refocus." He laughed when he said that, and it was apparent that he wasn't sure of the logic in that whole "readjustment" idea. I imagined his wife as I smiled. Maybe a large, friendly woman, looking after the kids pretty much alone and wondering about her old man on rainy nights, like this one. I felt sorry for his family, as he was a man on his own.

"Naw, hell, I hate bein' away from them all the time, but the road gets in your blood, y'know?" I nodded manfully, as if the road was in my blood already. "It's the only thing I been doin'

32

for the past twenty-three years, and I *can't* just up and leave it."
I looked at his forty-something face, tried to calculate his age
when he started, felt a bit numb.

"...with my daddy in '42, when I was nineteen years old. I missed
the draft 'cause we was haulin' loads 'necessary for the war
effort.' We didn't have hydraulic seats in them days, neither!"
He laughed. He had been at it that long and was not all that
colorful. I was in love with his family, sad at his plight, pleased
with his honesty, worried about the time.

At last he shoved himself sideways out of his chair and headed
for the bathroom again. "Last call before we go," he solemnly
announced, and I followed him into the john for our final duty
before climbing back aboard.

Back on the highway, it was pleasant in the high cab, out of the
rain, with the beast fleeing west at a surprising speed after the
coffee shop. We were more than driver and rider now. Rather,
we were companions of the road, no longer needing to shout
inane, simple statements across the console, but commenting
only on those things that suited us. I began to understand the
rasping CB radio, and my driver shared some of the meaning
behind the colorful language. The rain gradually dissolved and
the sun broke through, very low, below the clouds. I was, at the
same moment, in love with and frightened by the broad
expanse before me and the wet warm heart of the earth at the
roadside. I was thrilled by the orange sun: highlighting the
bellies of the clouds above us and warming me as no manmade
heater could. The signs for Elkhart hove into sight, and I felt
childishly happy in the silence of our roar and the damp earth
around us. My driver began to downshift, gears and differential,

as he had two hours before, but in my imagining, without so much of the kicking and pulling of the earlier pit stop.

I reached for my pack and felt a wave of warm glee as I basked in our friendship and the new kinship I had for the road.

Turning to shake hands, however, I found the driver intent on the hazards of his narrow pull-off, and he only quickly shook my hand and unexpectedly shouted, "Good luck, pal!" We were shouting again, and I fell from the side of the monster with my head in confusion. I reached up and slammed the door from below with a loud "So long!" but he was pulling away with a lashing of gears before I lifted my pack again. My eyesight quivered.

Turning to the road, I stuck out my thumb at the first auto and realized that I'd left my sign with the driver of the insulation rig headed for a house trailer factory in Elkhart, Indiana. I felt pleased with my forgetfulness, a gift to my friend, although I'm sure that the cardboard which read "WEST" ended up in the trash of that plant, along with the thousands of tons of other scrap from that impermanent place.

Chapter Nine

Elk Heart

The wind across the plains hits the northern Midwestern states as an angry god. I was standing in the on-ramp of a forlorn turnpike exit, west of Elkhart, Indiana, and that vengeful god was whipping my back like I was a rented mule. I became thick-headed as the weather blew by, and I thought only of getting a ride out of this forsaken place and leaving the grim-mouthed farmers far behind in the night. But of course, they were in no mood to give help to a straggly-looking character who was rather obviously cursing them under his breath anyway. Time ground on.

I was slowly learning to hate Elkhart, Indiana. I was not fond of the *sound* of the name of the town to begin with, and to be dropped off in this dismal landscape was no improvement on my prejudice. However, to be standing on the edge of the disintegrating concrete, to be ignored by furrowed old men, and to be mercilessly punished for a crime of which I was not guilty? Well, this was just a bit too much. The hate built in me in a slow, permanent way, the blocks sliding into place in my wall with each passing four- or eighteen-wheeler. The sun dipped very low in the dark sky.

Cursing my luck and my stupidity at this frozen venture, I kicked rocks, did jumping jacks, screamed curses at the top of my lungs. I was freezing, dammit!!! I couldn't believe it. I screamed toward the autos after they rolled by: "I'm not a rapist, you asshole!" "I don't want your money, fucker, just gimme a *ride*!!!" I was becoming desperate. *"Aaaaaaaaahhhhhhhhhhh!!!"* Frustrated, cold, and (unwilling to admit it) frightened. The prospects grew worse as the darkness groped for me and the State Patrol periodically drove past. The officers eyed me coldly, studying my pack for telltale signs, sizing me up. I mumbled only under my breath toward them. I put on every stitch of clothing I had, including a pair of not-too-clean athletic socks over my hands.

The sun finally did drop over the edge of the distant trees, and the cold became earnest. *"Shiiiiiiiiiiiiiiiit!!!"* I was screaming. My first day on the *real* road, the one out of Ohio, and here I was stuck near the house trailer factory in Elkhart, Indiana. What a slap in the face! The wind punctuated my thoughts. I passed in cycles between extreme calm and extreme frustration. The police had frightened me out of crossing the magic line dividing the on-ramp from the turnpike, the officious toll booths glowing in the gathering dusk, dividing me from the main artery of my desires. I was angry with them all, even in their not speaking to me, and I did not want to hear them speak. I was freezing in silence.

After what seemed unendurable hours, I numbly pawed my pack on and began to stumble toward the mouth of the on-ramp, back toward civilization. I could see the classic roadside plastic-joint near the turnpike entrance, the neon so out-of-place among the dark fields that it was visible for miles. My hands were numb inside of the white socks I had pulled over them. I slipped the bag over my shoulder and struggled toward the dark strip of the two-lane. It seemed a very long walk, with my feet growing impossibly colder, my legs distant, my cheeks buzzing with the cold. I was in hope that the walk would warm me up, the same way that all hitchhikers begin to fantasize impossibilities when left in one place too long.

Reaching the state two-lane, I began the tedious plod over the bridge to the lights of the orange, unnatural motel-gas station-coffee shop. I stopped halfway. Looking over the edge of the tubular metal guardrail on the low bridge walls, I could see the traffic entering the pool of light at the ramp intersection and then quickly pass into the darkness and then back into the light from under the bridge I was standing on. I contemplated numbers. I realized that the State Patrol had an office nearby, as there were too many of them passing up and down, like bees around a hive, to mean anything else. I counted the number of cars passing under me, subtracting those which entered from the ramp. It was a bit staggering. The traffic on the ramp was pathetic, so weak they didn't even justify *having* a ramp here, considering how few people used it. I became enraged at the engineers for putting in this ridiculous ramp, spending millions of dollars, when it got such little use but caused so much pain. I cursed low and evenly, long strings of the foulest stuff I could conjure.

The cursing cheered me immensely.

I had, of course, long ago decided what I would do. And the time spent counting cars was merely a build-up. I was watching the police, and they were watching me whenever they went by. The observations led me to think I might be able to predict a time when they wouldn't be rolling past.

Finally, and with great resolve, I walked back to the end of the bridge and slung my pack over the edge. I allowed my bag to drop from my hands and prayed as it rolled a bit down the grassy hill, half expecting it to roll to the pavement below and to my left. When it stopped, and I considered it the very best moment, when I knew no cops were imminent, I slung a leg

37

over the abutment, putting it inside the fence line and therefore making my leg illegal. Just as I was in the midst of cursing the engineer who had rigged the barbed wire against anyone jumping down toward the highway, I spotted another patrolman on his way out of the toll booth and headed toward me on the off-ramp. He drove at a good clip. "Damn!" This night was not going my way.

Whipping my illegal appendage back up, I childishly readied myself with an absurd lie. I began to walk fearfully toward the neon lights again, which immediately punched holes in my story: "I was just propping my pack on the top of the guardrail, when I bumped it over, and…. " "But I was just going to retrieve my pack, sir, I *need* that stuff!" I was angry, humiliated, nervous, and still strolling away from my goods as the officer rounded the corner and came toward me on the bridge. I steeled myself for the flashing lights or maybe even the loudspeaker. I knew that I would come clean with him, that I wouldn't lie as I'm so weak at it. And that I would probably not have a very peaceful night for the rest of my wait on the on-ramp.

I even went so far as to envision a warm night in the county lock-up, although I immediately dismissed this as impossible.

He sped by without glancing.

Gleeful, grinning, heedless of the cold, I continued in the same direction until the patrol car was out of sight. Turning, I raced back to the edge of the bridge and, with a quick glance, dropped over the concrete into the cold dark grass. I slipped, sat down hard, and slid on my hindquarters down toward my pack. As I reached for it in the night, I felt the thrill of my heart, my breathing fast and joyful. I didn't speak but rather silently celebrated my disobedience. I was so happy to be on the other side of the fence, no longer hemmed in to the dreariness of Elkhart, Indiana, but on the side of the fence toward freedom, and the open road, and the West.

Walking back into the bubble of light in the bridge area, I readied myself with an innocent story designed to free me from the cops, should I fall into their unfeeling hands. The story, of course, was as idiotic as the last tale I had conjured, and I actually knew, deep-down, that no one in their right mind would ever believe it. However, the innocence of the story, the childishness of my folly, would surely make the patrolman smile and overlook my indiscretion... I was sure of it.

Near the bridge abutment and the end of the on-ramp, I hopped nervously from foot-to-foot, waiting for the flashing lights of the Highway Patrol or else the welcome slowing of one of the autos speeding so near my elbow. I felt rushes of illegal glee running up my legs, tightening my bowels, forcing my hands to shake. I could also feel the warmth of the inside of one of those cars, and I had faith that the policeman would let me go back to the on-ramp should he catch me here half-hiding.

I was just tiring of my illicit thrill and had grown callous to my new standing-spot already, due to the cold and wind... I was not paying attention, not the way one should under these circumstance... I was looking at my feet, contemplating their numbness, when suddenly I heard the gravel popping and my heart was in my throat. I was speechless with terror at being arrested, knew that the police were here and so *soon*!

My innocent panic flushed quickly into shaky relief when I finally realized I had snagged a ride. That I had succeeded, finally, in getting a ticket out of this god-forsaken place. I was jubilant.

39

I knew, of course, that I would need someone crazy if he was going to stop on the turnpike at night. No one picks up grubby-looking characters after dark on the immensely freezing, utterly illegal turnpike, *especially* after dark. But I wasn't quite ready for what was within.

The guy in the car was a loud-speaking shaman, recently sprung from the bowels of a rock-and-roll joint in Elkhart. He was in the midst of a loud ritual when he pulled over, and I became more aware of just how loud as I hustled my pack toward his door. But I wasn't prepared for the blast which swept past me when he popped open the passenger rear door. It was incredible. I was aware immediately of the smell: stale beer mixed with fresh beer, a deep animal stink, and thick pungent marijuana smoke. My mouth watered as I loaded my pack in the back and then slapped into the front seat.

Yeah, I knew that it had to be someone crazy so it might as well be this shaggy brute, and we lurched onto the highway with the deep roar of spilled gravel. We raced through the gears and topped the speed limit in less than seventy-five seconds. Looked like a lot of fast miles in store tonight.

I ground my frozen fingers against each other, and I turned, while blowing on them, and smiled at the rapidly fading lights of the highway on-ramp for Elkhart, Indiana. I thought of the truck driver and his all–American life.

Turning back to the dude with the hair and shaggy coat, I laughingly thanked him and, using his church key, popped open a beer. I took a deep, unfelt swallow, jammed my feet underneath his heating duct, puffed on the thin joint. He roared at me about American Indians, about "shape shifters" or something like that, on and on in unintelligible semi-native bursts.

I smiled childishly at our seventy-mile-per-hour society. I leaned back, feeling my muscles and my pain, and worked on a new high. I spoke quietly to the driver: "It's so fucking easy to be an outlaw in this country." He, of course, could not hear me, did not even glance my way, but howled his song, bugling the refrain over and over. He belted out the words to the song and burned a hole in the dark American night.

Chapter Ten

Wolf Man

The beasts of the night are never so terrible as when they pilot ton-heavy armor and flash across the land at unholy speed. Thus did the man with a rock-and-roll high skip us across the broad, flat, black American night toward the city lights of Chicago, through the flames and horror of Gary, Indiana.

My pilot, following great initial bursts of confusing American Indian references, turned out to be not much of a talker, and the music wound us through the blackness without the need for conversation. His hair flopping forward and back, his nails white over the hard roundness of the steering wheel, and his glassy eyes hard on the road lines whipping below us. He was a creature of the night, and was alive with the anticipation of a killer night in the jungles of Chicago, his home and hideaway.

"Elkhart!!" He howled to me again and again through the screams of his radio. "I eat that shit for breakfast, man! Ain't nothin' in Elkhart but *trailers!*" He found this the funniest thing in the universal night and pounded on the wheel, losing himself in the high, and then slowly regressed to his task of guiding us to the heart of Chicago. His eyes again gripped the road, gleaming in the passing lights. Firm, bold, and resolute in his intent.

He dropped me off in the middle of the city without a word, his lips fairly quivering with anticipation of a bloody wild night. As soon as I pulled my pack out of the backseat, he was off with a roar, the stink and howling and noise tunneling into the night.

After reading *On the Road*, I had wanted nothing more than to experience "bop at the loop," and I'd had fantasies about mixing in with the after-beats and hippies. But in the reality of the cold, confusing, loud, illuminated night, I felt frightened and wanted only to find my way out.

I still give thanks that I didn't have to wait long for the next ride.

I snaked away from that place in the company of a slow, quiet old man headed for pastoral Wisconsin, and fell into fitful sleep, jerking awake again and again, with dreams of dogs tearing at my throat. Merciful, if fitful, sleep until the gratitude of morning.

As dawn slowly crept up behind us, I gradually realized that I had passed my first test. That I had completed the first cycle of my infantile journey. I found myself alive, growing stronger, and capable in facing the simple task of crossing a virginal state. I began to feel more alive and more capable than I had previously imagined.

I was on my way.

Chapter Eleven

The Loosest Man in the World

I finally met up with Michael in Minnesota. He had been in Michigan visiting some family, and we had decided to meet at my old school-friend's parents' home, in a small town outside the Twin Cities on a date late in March. Of course, he was two days late, and I had an uncomfortable time of it, trying to hold on to my meager funds while also having a good time with friends. My Minnesota friend Tom Bauer and I enjoyed a couple of evenings after he was done with work, and as his folks were very loving, I was well-fed for a change.

All was in anticipation as Mike's reputation preceded him: handsome, bold, fun, outrageous, otherworldly… I told my friends all about him for the two days before he arrived. Tom arranged little gatherings for us during my stay there, and each evening we expected Mike's arrival. After I'd exhausted my "outrageous Mike" stories, we tried to focus on other things: discussions of canoeing in the Boundary Waters, whatever was on TV, what the coming year was bringing, and on and on, Michael's shadow always at our elbow as we awaited his arrival. The final night, a big crowd of Tom's friends gathered at his folks' house, hoping once again to meet the phantom vagabond.

Mike's arrival was dramatic, loud, and exciting, as always. The manner of his entering our quiet group left the complacency of the past two days a memory. We had all been waiting for him, and we had already given up on him for this particular evening as it was late. We were sitting around quietly talking in the Bauers' front room when he burst, roaring, upon the scene.

When we opened the door, I was half-afraid to see who might be knocking so long after dark, and sure enough, Mike was there, his raggedy appearance setting me at once into mixed laughter, relief, and anger. He, of course, was stone drunk.

"Hey!… Hi!… Hi!… Hi!… *Eddie*!! He was shaking hands all around, booming with laughter and beaming a toothsome grin, shaking off the straps of his pack and shuffling into the house against the crowd of bodies near the door.

The contrast was striking, between the rather clean-cut appearance of the folks from Minnesota and this curly-headed bum that had stumbled in the door. Mike was still grinning his rather drunken smile and all the while talking, saying hello over and over again, and trying to tell us how he happened to arrive in this state at this hour. I fell to the edge of the group to observe and to try to make sense of the commotion.

"Well, I was in town before nine o'clock," he started, half-shouting, half-laughing, "but I was with this ca-razy young guy, see, and he felt like havin' a beer, so we went over to the… well, ah… the Star Bar, or something like that, and we had a few beers, and then I told him I was tryin' to save money for the trip, and then he was buyin' the beer, and of course he wanted to hear all about where we're goin' because he's never been there, and so we just kept talkin' and drinkin' and tellin' stories, and…" Here Mike was no longer able to contain his laughter, and he let it all spill out, drawing us all into it and, at the same time, doing a quick scan for a refrigerator.

"Uh, say, do you guys have any beer around here?" He was laughing again, having asked for beer in someone's house whom he had never really met, and he was so alive and pleasantly smashed that he had the whole room simply cackling with his innocent humor. On the other hand, I'm that guy who slips to the edge of the group when there's a lot going on, and I stood there now.

The similarities were striking, too. I was surprised at how at home Mike appeared, with his blondish hair curling down over his eyes, and his slim, six-foot frame fitting in with the athletic crowd of Minnesotans. I was laughing, too, at both the similarities and the differences between him and the quiet, non-alcoholic and gentle people who were receiving him so warmly. It was a delight.

Someone did produce a beer, and Michael tipped it up, letting the beer gurgle in his throat, with a little foam at the corners of his mouth, until he had to stop for breath, tears in his eyes. He paused, and a low, rippling belch echoed through the room, and once again we were all laughing loudly. He finally turned to me (hovering at the edge of the group), and we shook hands, pounded backs, and had a nice welcome between us.

Finally, with the entrance festivities over and a few words to calm things down a bit, Mike looked things over, assessing where we were and how soon we'd be leaving. The circle of clean faces stared back at him with amused respect.

He was feeling frisky.

"Well, ah, what have you guys been doing tonight? I mean, are you doing anything tonight?"

There were a few women in the room, and they still seemed to have the giggles over this madman, and Mike looked at them pointedly for a moment. "Uh, well... really, what have you been doing?" He turned to look at me, and I smiled in the rather uneasy silence that was growing in the room.

"Look, Mikey, why don't ya just sit down for a while and relax?" I was speaking to him kindly. "We'll be taking off in the morning, and we've just been sitting here talking and taking it easy tonight. Sort of waiting around to see if you'd show up or not. And people have to work tomorrow."

"Oh, uh… yah, well, yah, sure." He looked at me knowing already that we would for *sure* have to cut out before too long, as he seemed a little unsure about the group hosting us.

I was grateful then for what is one of Mike's greatest attributes: he is accepting and loving of everyone he meets, at least until they wrong him. Although he arrived hoping for a party, he smiled hugely, settled into a chair, and, tipping his head back, let the rest of the beer gurgle down his throat.

"Well, yes, how are you all doing? What's your names?" And so the tail end of the evening was underway, with someone bringing Michael a couple more beers that he didn't ask for, but which he slurped down gratefully. He was a charmer for this night, letting the tension of his electric entrance ease into a comfortable conversation which had been the mood before his arrival. After a few stories, and some laughter, and getting clear that the few women were firmly attached to other fellas in the room, Mike began to shut down for the night as did the rest of us.

Most of the folks left, girding their loins for a tired day of work the next day.

"Well, Eddie, I'm glad to see you, man!" We shook hands in the dark and relaxed a little more as we let the evening sink into our eyes and hearts.

"Yeah, well, Mike, you son-of-a-bitch, I've been waiting for you for two days, man."

He giggled. "Aaahhh, Eddie..." He let this comment trail off, as he did so often.

We finished out the evening with a little talk of plans and money, and finally, crawling into our sleeping bags (which seemed so foreign and smelly in this clean house), we fell into a snore.

Mike had again, in his inimitable fashion, talked me into *not* making any plans for the next day, just leaving things in the air until we were good and ready to go. I fell into a loose and comfortable sleep, my body accepting the wooden floor as if it were my bed at home. Our host, Tom Bauer, was already into his work-sleep, and we all smiled as we dreamed the remainder of the night away.

Chapter Twelve

Graduation

Tom Bauer woke me early in the morning to say goodbye and I, hardly recognizing him, mumbled my thanks and rolled over. I slept until late in the morning, readying my body for what was to come. When I'd finally gotten up, stowed my gear, and had a (last!?) shower, I found my way to the kitchen. There I found Mom Bauer and Michael in a comfortable morning conversation; she putzing with breakfast, him commenting between sips of coffee. Tom's mother was obviously smitten by Michael the vagabond, and she was enjoying this leisurely morning and the full attentions of such a rascal. She seemed on the verge of giddy. I felt awkward in their presence.

"Eddie!! You're late!!" Mike smiled a laughing smile, letting me know that his plans were still the same: "no plans is good plans."

Mom Bauer was a great talker, too, and the time fled quickly. I thought I was hiding my anxiety well but felt like I was sitting on an anthill. Mike, on the other hand, seemed more settled into the house with each passing minute.

"Listen, Mike... uhh... when were you thinkin' about leaving?" I sounded as casual as I could make it. My studied tone only amplified my unease.

"Eddie! Any time, man, any time." He paused, then loudly: "Don't worry!!" He turned back to his coffee. Mrs. B. was busy getting ready to go.

When we finally loaded the car, Mike and the Missus jabbering away the whole time, she had a final thought: "Listen, I'm sorry, but there's just one stop I need to make before I take you boys up to the freeway." I climbed into the backseat, squirming and impatient, but Mikey, up front, was easy and fluid. He just accepted the day as it unfolded.

We ended up at the Lutheran church rummage sale.

Tom's mom was a real garage-sale/rummage-sale fiend. She took off like a shot when we got to the church basement, knowing exactly what she was hunting for. I moped along, cursing my luck. "Godammit, Mike, when are we gonna get *going*?" I was near hopping, impatient as a puppy, tugging at the road like it was a chew rag.

"Eddie, look, man, it's gonna be cold out there, so look around and find yourself some extra stuff. And we'll get on the road when the time is right." He was right, of course: the extra clothes I carried with me would fit in a shoebox. I was deflated instantly and began to look around the long tables for warmth.

At last, with two holey sweaters and a new knit cap (total cost: thirty cents), Mike and I jumped eagerly into the auto with Mom B. (who had purchased an absolutely *tiny* TV), and the outward journey began.

Naturally, our timing was exactly right, and we were pulling away with a ride before Mrs. Bauer had turned around. She was my last connection to anything I'd known in my youth. Waving to her out the back window of the car as if from a nursery, I felt my last attachment to the world, as I knew it, fall behind me. I turned carefully around to face the wide-open, middle distance of the unknown.

Chapter Thirteen

Baby Steps

Our first ride together, so quickly claimed after Mom B. dropped us off, was with a youngish, very dull fellow that we later referred to as "Dim Jim." He was headed considerably west, into the wide open spaces of western Minnesota and eastern North Dakota. He asked us within a few miles if we'd chip in for gas, to which Mikey, his heart as big as the world, immediately replied, "Yes." Jim soon pulled over, collected money from us both, and then filled up the tank. We rolled westward through a great, very plain land, with little to distract us. Unexpectedly, our driver wheeled off the highway and into the squeaky-clean town of St. Cloud, and, to our delight, we were treated as welcome guests at some distant relatives of Jim's... great, hearty, Midwestern food was provided all around, and Mike, glorying in his *On the Road*-ness, shouted, "...and throw some beans in it!!" which was apparently understood only by the two of us. After TV and talk, we packed back into Jim's sedan and rolled again, the low sun to our port bow, the vacant land broken mostly by the radio, which thankfully still received over the long distances between cities.

As we approached Fargo, Jim began to make noise about money again. Mike and I, without talking about it, had assumed that our earlier donation was a one-time thing. Being passive as I was, I was grateful to be in the backseat as Mike quietly explained that we had very little money and wouldn't be able to keep feeding the horse. I guess that Jim figured we owed him, what with the relatives feeding us and all, and he became visibly sullen and silent behind the wheel. When he turned on his blinker to get off the highway, we exchanged a few words, him vaguely suggesting that he needed to visit other family here, alone, and we clarifying that we needed to keep moving. So we parted company then and there.

It was a relief to get out of the car and away from Jim, and the fresh air momentarily refreshed us. However, the cold gradually closed a cramped hand around us, despite our new-used sweaters, and we were once again hungry for the comfort of a heated interior.

We managed just one more ride that evening, thankfully all the way across town to the west side of Fargo. We stood on the west on-ramp until things really got cold and dark. Walking to the only gas station within sight, we inquired if we might pitch our tent behind the station where there was a decent patch of grass. The attendant, obviously not the owner, "…could give a shit!" And so as the day turned to dark, I busied myself with laying the horrid bright-orange poncho-groundsheet down then staking out the tiny tent. Mike being unfamiliar with the task just watched this first time. I was strangely emotional as I did the work, breathing very heavy through my mouth, really on the verge of tears. I still remember those ten minutes to this day and don't know what that was about: perhaps it was the cold and my attending fear; perhaps it was the sense of loneliness of us on our own in this forlorn setting; perhaps (being the sensitive type) I perceived the attendant's comments being that he didn't give a shit about *me*. Whatever the cause, I bared quite a lot of heavy breathing, enough that Mike commented on it the next day.

However, once inside the tent, my loneliness vanished, and with our sleeping bags warming us, and the tent so tiny that our body heat reflected back and forth, we soon dropped off to sleep in anticipation of a bright morning.

Chapter Fourteen

Growing Warmer

As dreamt-of, the morning was bright and clear, although snapping cold. Having fallen asleep very early we were up with first dawn, and as not even the gas station was open, we stumbled to the freeway without benefit of either food or coffee. I felt grateful for the big afternoon meal of the day before as it was tiding us over.

We had on every bit of clothing that we owned, even considered draping our sleeping bags over us but thought this might look too odd and be too cumbersome for getting into a car. So instead we stood hitching as bundled as we could be, our packs resting at our sides. Mike and I weren't your average "couldn't-care-less" type of hitchhikers. Despite Mikey being larger-than-life to me, he joined me in being very deliberate about trying to reel in rides: stand where there's a pull-off, straighten yourself up as best you can, look the driver in the eye, and *smile*! I still believe that this was a key to many a driver pulling over for us... we didn't look like bums or rapists.

During the long, orange-colored wait, we began to wonder how it was that we were hitchhiking in the North, in the spring... why had we not headed south to warmer climes? In fact, we had no answer, other than we'd identified a place to meet that was far north... although we joked about it at the time, we kicked ourselves for not thinking this through. We were childish in our planning. However, we gave no thought to turning south now as we were onboard for the big cycle, a tour around our great country, and it was either the big loop or else nothing.

This did little to warm us in the cold sun.

Finally, we hitched a ride with another young man, this one considerably brighter than Dim Jim, who was happy to give us a ride and was headed to Bismarck. I was relieved when he didn't ask us for money, and we had a lively chat along the way. Happily, our driver needed coffee not too long into the ride, and we were able to fill up on gut-bomb donuts, too, relieving our hunger. With a much brighter outlook, we continued west.

Chapter Fifteen

How We Got By

From an Interview in 2010

"I left my family's home with fifty-five-dollars cash, and that money lasted me a good long time. I need to be honest and say that of that fifty-five dollars, I spent more of it on beer than I did on food or anything else, so you can see how my priorities were back then. I also picked up work along the way: offloading lumber, working as a waiter, and even on a railroad crew as a gandy dancer. (But I found that they treated me just the same as those poor black fellas, so I walked away after a couple of days without ever getting paid.) So, we got by on very little.

"After a few states, I (or even better, Michael), would fall into a little rhythm, asking very casually near sundown: 'Do you know a good place that we could camp around here?' or 'Where can we get a meal real cheap around here?' Sometimes the driver did know, and he'd drop us off at what he thought was a good place, but other times the driver would mull it over. The trick at this moment is to remain quiet and let the driver think about us, about his home situation, his spiritual life, and on like that. If we hit pay dirt, the driver would just take us home, or sometimes we'd wait outside while our driver went in to talk it over with the wife, and we enjoyed many a meal from good Christian strangers in this way. The best thing was when we'd get dinner, as well as breakfast, if the ride worked out that way, and so we would be pretty fueled up for the next day or so. I have tried, in my new life, to repay kindnesses such as these by helping strangers when I can.

"When we did break down and buy a meal, it was usually at one of those places that serves breakfast all day. We ended up at a chain called Sambo's on several occasions, although those folks went out of business at the same time the book of the same name disappeared from the book-scape. I feel alright about that, as I never was comfortable with that whole 'Little Black Sambo' reference at the eatery. Anyhow, the reason we'd choose breakfast is that you could get a pile of food cheap... we were all about quantity in those days, much less focused on the quality. Our mantra was 'Eat Everything!' and so down went pancakes with all the butter and syrup we could get on there... two eggs were always on the order, and as long as the waitress would keep bringing coffee, we'd keep pouring the milk and sugar in and keep drinking it for nutrition. More than once a waitress finally stopped coming to the table, so tired she'd become of us just sitting there consuming. We'd always leave at least something of a tip though, knowing how it was to get by as a waiter or other bottom-rung worker.

"Now, crashing at friends' places was always a little tricky... we'd designed a couple routes to hit friends' (or even friends' parents') places: Tom in the Twin Cities, Paul in Tempe, the Bakers outside of Los Gatos, Judy and her sister in Redondo Beach, and others... but the trick was to visit and absorb without making ourselves unwanted. Tom's mom, so concerned for me when she saw me, tried to give me money which I refused. She finally wore down to physically pressing one dollar into my hand, saying 'A lucky dollar. It's a lucky dollar! I *want* you to have it.' And I kept that dollar for the longest time, sometimes in my shoe if things looked dicey.

"But mostly we'd just make do as we went along, camping beside the road or, when in the West, walking into the national forest to bed down. In Oregon, Mike and I became so enamored of a little campsite under Mount Hood that we just stayed there for days. I walked into town twice just to buy eggs for us to cook out in the woods.

"Two places stand out in my mind: one is the Russian River in Northern California. For some reason, perhaps as a result of our clever questioning process, we got dropped off there and just crawled under the wire fence and spent two days enjoying ourselves. The other is a beach area right on the Oregon-California border, where dozens of young folks car-camped. Very generous, lovely folks, to a person, and they were constantly of a mood to share. We lingered there, enjoying the cooked food and the ample wine and marijuana of the place, a little slice of unsanctioned heaven.

"Now, an unexpected place to get cheap food is a hospital. The only reason I know this is that during one ride where there were two drivers, one of them started having trouble with her eyes... became convinced that she needed to have a doctor look at them. It was a small town and we had a long, dreary wait for the right doc to arrive... in part to kill time, I wandered to the canteen in the basement. Instead of the nasty cafeteria food I was expecting, I found another little slice of heaven in the low-cost, high-quality fare they provided. I thereafter sought out hospitals when I could and have not been disappointed. The problem a hitchhiker faces is, at least in those days, the hospitals were near the center of town, and most times I was traveling down the highway, trying to avoid the congestion and short rides associated with urban areas. But when possible...

"Cleanliness was a challenge, as you might imagine. When visiting friends, we'd get cleaned up good, but for long stretches we were without decent hygiene. I sometimes wonder what the drivers thought who'd pick us up after a stretch of camping in the woods. We'd try to rinse off in a creek, but man that water can be an icy challenge, especially in the morning. But I usually carried a very small bottle of cleanser with me, not too particular what kind, and we'd sometimes wash hair and pits, sometimes our underwear in a creek. Of course I wouldn't do that kind of thing now, what with the environmental awareness and all, but getting that layer of grime, road dust, exhaust fumes, and sweat off once in a while was a mighty refreshing treat.

"I was good at scavenging small things like little bars of soap and makeshift rolls of toilet paper whenever I could, as sometimes the choices you face are all unhappy ones. I've had to wipe my butt with discarded paper bags, bits of cloth, leaves, and the like. Of course like old-timey people, I'd use the water in a creek sometimes, but like I said before, I wouldn't do that now. But you *know* you're in sad shape when you gotta use pine needles or the like. One time in Washington State, I wasn't watching what I was doing and scratched my ass with a plant that I later discovered is called Devil's Paw. Man, for two days after that I could hardly sit!

"But, like I said, mostly we just made it up as we went along. If we got rattled or didn't know what to do, we'd just go to the nearest café and sit there and drink coffee and grill the waitress about our best options... you'd be amazed at how well that works. But mostly, the luck was just given... there is some kind of goodness in just having trust in the Lord to take care of you."

Chapter Sixteen

North Dakota

Minnesotans have little jokes about people from North Dakota. I still remember a couple and still get a laugh with them now and then: "Somebody threw away a perfectly good South Dakotan!!" gets 'em every time.

The low, sullen hills of North Dakota have a way of taking the starch out of you. As we headed west, slowly conquering the long land, we became troubled and sullen from the lack of inspiration in the world. We passed Bismarck without actually seeing it, the highway going *around* the capital of the state. I reflected on stories that my dad told of living there for one year when he was part of an itinerant labor family: one was that someone had given them venison, and the winter was so cold, they simply hung it on the porch and sawed chunks off for dinner.

I felt the life in me slowly pulsate up and down, sometimes feeling the thrill of moving so quickly over so much space, only to lapse again into the disgruntled aimlessness of making so much trouble over such boring prospects as the Dakotas. Mike and I sometimes quarreled. We behaved like the adolescents we were, the words spilling out hot and angry over the smallest problems. Yet we were stuck and we knew it. I found him intolerable at times, and he me. We traveled with salesmen who didn't seem to care where they were going. We looked out at land that was fertile, pimply with new crops, the product of last year's seed, and gradually it all blurred together into one. The whole arrangement seemed intolerable in a way: we were stuck with each other, and we were stuck with these pointless old men, and even though others *told* us we were headed in the right direction, it seemed impossible that we would ever get "there." I felt that my pack was too heavy. I felt that Mike's pack was too light. I thought that the drivers were unknowledgeable and uncooperative, as they never seemed to go quite the distance I wanted. Unfortunately, Mike felt the same, so we were constantly at odds.

It really took the starch out of you.

Finally, however, we began to see the distance fall behind us on the map. I became acutely aware of that map and the different instruments used to calculate our progress: a bit of a pack strap, a fingernail, a piece of torn paper, a knife blade. Anything and everything became the measuring tools of our progress, became the promise of something more, and I found myself wanting to measure every twenty minutes. Mike was patient with me.

The hours trod slowly by, with us either looking into the faces of curious bovines or cramming ourselves and our gear into the back of lavish Pontiacs. Once our driver had a CB radio and tried to connect us for a ride with a trucker, but the truckers only wanted "beaver" and we felt our fate sealed by the gender between our legs.

Once a Cadillac... that was a real pleasure. The driver was half-asleep, and despite the lavish vehicle (or maybe *because* of it: so quiet and comfortable), we were curiously bored. Then at long last, we began to measure, with forgetful, adult, and unforgiving eyes, that the distance to the next state line was no larger than the nail of my right index finger. Then no bigger than the tip of a knife. Then we were there.

61

It seemed as if there was no time left. It looked as if there was no time behind us: the waiting, the riding, and even the time beneath the largest cow in the world. (Years later: "Yeah, Eddie, do you remember the biggest cow in the world, out there with all the lights on it on top of that hill in the middle of North Dakota?" "Yeah, I remember. We slept almost underneath that fucker, how could I forget it?") It felt as if all the slow times in-between seemed to fall behind, and it had fallen behind really without either of us noticing it, and we had grown without either of us seeing it. Our childhood was falling behind us, and now we were on the border of Montana, without anything but ourselves and our bags and our maps.

Chapter Seventeen

Big Sky Country

Anyone entering the Rocky Mountain States... Montana, Wyoming, Colorado, New Mexico... from the east is profoundly disappointed to find no mountains there. I've heard it from others, and it was certainly true for me, that I expected to see mountains the moment I crossed the border into a Mountain State, and especially the one named Montana. Really, all we saw was the great expanse of the sky above, the pale green of the land below, and a thin line where they met in the distance. It was an empty place, alright.

Now, I'm sure that we had adventures in Montana, but I didn't write down much of anything. Besides what little I wrote, there's only three things that stand out in my mind. Number one is the first ambiguous sight we had of the distant peaks. I happened to be riding in the front, which was kind of rare for me, with an older, graying, chubby local man who had picked us up at a no-name exit and would later drop us off at another no-name exit. The morning was clear, the sun behind us, and the white clouds in the distance seemed an aberration... they just didn't look right. I kept peering at them (I wear glasses now, and I suppose I needed them then.), trying not to be too naïve in thinking they were mountains. I peered and peered, the car silent as we rolled along, and I was defeated in my attempt to connect the white clouds to any land mass below. My mind flipped back and forth: "Mountains... clouds... no, mountains." Later: "No, they're clouds." Finally, I could contain myself no longer and simply blurted out to the driver: "Are those clouds up ahead there?" He smiled a long smile toward me. Mike, who had been half-asleep in the backseat, suddenly sat forward.

"No, son, those are mountaintops." They were pure white with snow on this spring morning, and beautiful laces of pale blue coursed through them.

The peaks were disembodied: floating, unattached, miraculous. They fairly sparkled in the sun, even at that great distance. We'd finally made it to the mountainous West! Here at last was the Promised Land. Here at last was a view of adulthood. No matter what happened after this, we could claim to have made it to the mountains. Life would never be the same.

I was elated. I can feel that elation in the bottom of my tummy, just telling you the story.

The second memory is the story of Crazy Woman... a range of those mountains we passed through, as well as a creek flowing out of the mountains, are named after a woman who either wandered away from or was left behind by her wagon train in the 1800s. She was found alone and babbling incoherently by a later wagon train, and the area in which she was found now bears a memory of her to this day.

The two stories are in such contrast to me: my own deliverance, my own redemption in finally attaining these shining mountains, and that poor woman's utter undoing by them, just one hundred years earlier. I have to confess that at the time, I was bewildered by the story... there was nothing I wanted more than to lose myself in such pristine, clean, beautiful country. But now that I'm older, I can see how an enforced solitude, fear of hunger and predators, and the utter unknowing of what would become of oneself would probably drive me around the bend now.

I doubt that I'll ever have a mountain range named after me, though.

The third is an event that Michael never forgave me for. You have to recall that we had very little money, and food was an irregular treat for us. Somewhere along the lonely highway in Montana, Mike announced, "You know as well as I do that we need some bulk, right? Let's get something to eat!" We walked off the highway into a little town that had a grocery and, after agonizing for some time, purchased a head of lettuce. I couldn't face the prospect of eating the lettuce on its own, so I insisted on the extravagance of a little bottle of salad dressing to help us eat it. Out on the highway, we used our knife to carefully cut the head in half. Placing one of the halves back in its sack, we cut the remaining half into half again, thus giving both of us a quarter of a head of lettuce to eat for that day. We doused them with dressing and immediately ate everything. The next day, we carefully cut the remaining half in half again, doused, and ate again. And this is where the crime occurred: after eating every last little green wisp of lettuce, we still had an inch of dressing in the bottom of the bottle. I saw this as sustenance, and although Michael begged me not to do it, I tipped the bottle up and slowly glugged the thick dressing down. Mikey nearly retched at the time and nearly retched any time the subject was mentioned ever after that.

Hunger'll do things to a young man like that.

Chapter Eighteen

Camping

As mentioned, we camped, and even if it was behind a church or a gas station, we almost always slept out. One of the most startling things for me, coming from a non-camping background, was the condition of most every "non-sanctioned" campsite we used.

I was shocked when a great bear of a driver in a battered Chevy Suburban informed us that you could camp anywhere you wanted in the national forest. The thought had never occurred to me. What little camping I had done was in developed campgrounds where you paid to have a clean site, water provided, and a vault toilet. Michael and I soon became expert at ferreting out good, free spots to sleep in the forest, but the trashy conditions in these places remains a mystery to me today. Anywhere that a four-wheel-drive vehicle could reach would include a huge campfire ring or six, the fire sites filled with smashed glass, half-melted aluminum foil, and scorched beer cans. Invariably, these sites were littered with the detritus of a hundred drunks: millions of tiny multi-hued glass shards, hundreds of pull-tabs from beer cans, bits of wire, and string and rope of all descriptions hanging from every part of the nearby trees. Anything that could be nailed to a tree was punched full of holes (along with the tree itself), and the ground was littered with spent shotgun shells, deformed lead, and brass cartridges.

Most troubling, though, was the condition of the poor trees themselves: every branch within reach torn off, shaggy stumps chopped and hacked-at, and alarmingly huge, half-burned logs lying across the fire rings, their previous assailants having unsuccessfully tried to burn them in half using the fire itself. But most pitiful were the large, still-standing, living trees: their bark chopped and sawed-upon, chunks of their trunks missing. The hardened blood of these beautiful giants ran down their flanks: staining, proclaiming injustice, and at times even pooling at their feet.

I see these men in my mind's eye, chopping and shooting and sawing in rage at the nature around them. Why do we hack at nature so callously in our great land? What is it that drives us to smash the natural at hand? The crime scenes looked as if deranged ogres had smashed and burned in an effort to relieve their own pain.

To this investigator, the evidence pointed to loneliness: divorce from Mother, possibly divorce from the wife, and maybe divorce from one's self.

We did do our part to try to clean things up, but traveling so light as we did weren't able to haul anything out with us.

But perhaps the scenes are of my own making. Perhaps I gaze into a still pool of my own watery reflection. I thrash my way across the face of our beautiful nation, seeking, ever seeking for the outside to relieve my inside. Unable to reconcile the heaving tides within, I express my unspoken anger in a thousand cuts and jabs. The victim, always, is innocence, and in the forest, the innocence of nature.

Chapter Nineteen

Medicine Man

We ground westward through Montana, sleeping through the cold nights in the national forest in our tiny tent, waking shocked at the cold late spring. Billings fell far behind, and we entered real mountains, with the highway rising and falling, curling around hillsides, following the rivers. The cold nights had an impact on me. I started getting sick, a hot infection blooming in my throat. I felt wobbly during the day. We camped at Big Timber, and the wood was so wet we couldn't get a fire started. I was miserable. Mikey had us count out our money, which was pitiful, and then we talked a little about where a Greyhound station might be. I didn't want to turn back, but I couldn't go on as I was.

In a flash of brilliance, Mike guided us out of the forest and down to a road that paralleled the main highway. On it were the lonely lights of a little roadhouse. We made our way toward it, the promise of warmth and sustenance at hand.

The bar was tiny and smoky and had but few murmuring patrons. The light was amber, shot with red, and the music decidedly Country. We sat and enjoyed a bowl of chili each. The hot and spicy glop soothed my aching throat and warmed my chilled bones. We hardly looked up during the feast, not eating fast, mind you, restraining ourselves to enjoy every mouthful, and so we were silent for some time. We asked for more bread, and of course coffee, and used the bread to mop the last of the red out of the gray ceramic bowls which were ringed with maroon on the outside. Although we both longed for beers, these were too much of an extravagance. We sat and sat, lapping up the warm stale air, the distant company, the feeling of the heat in our bellies. Finally, after he had paid the bill, Mike poured half a shaker of salt into a napkin, folded it over several times to wrap the precious salt, and stuck it in his pocket.

Back at our dark, cold camp, Mike had me pour some of the salt into a cup and add water from my canteen. Following his direction, I tipped the cup up and repeatedly gargled the salt water. I thought at first I was going to retch, as I'd put way too much salt in the cup, but I was able to settle down and repeat the process several times. I slept like the dead that night and awoke cold, but the fire in my throat was noticeably less fierce. My head, although still a bit wobbly, ached less, and I felt optimism for the first time in a couple of days. We worked our way back down to the highway and continued west through the cold, unforgiving dawn.

We saw the turnoff for Boulder (first I knew that there was any "Boulder" other than the one in Colorado), and a sign for some hot springs there. I longed for the hot springs, but not knowing how far off the main road Boulder was, we kept on the highway.

We passed Bozeman, then Butte, then through the city of Missoula, which proved very friendly, providing our first reefer in many a day. Although we were now in June, the mornings remained very cold, and we bundled into our sleeping bags early every night, tired or not.

The mountains surrounding us were a constant wonder, a source of tremendous entertainment, every bend revealing a new view. I gained strength, and we had a sense of coming into our own. We fought less, conversed with our drivers a bit more, felt happy and directed.

So this is what growing up feels like!

Chapter Twenty

Crime and Punishment

Our final ride out of Montana was a doozy: traveling salesman, obviously a smart ass, nicely dressed, big CB antenna dominating the car from the top of the trunk. He was very chatty with us… and very chatty with the truckers on his CB radio… on and on, in language I could barely understand. He, like an earlier driver, tried to arrange for a trucker to pick us up where he planned to drop us, but again the freight haulers inevitably asked, "Is that a beaver or a dick?" and when the response was "dick," the other party invariably went silent. We crossed the border into the thin neck of Idaho.

Our driver, white shirt, bright tie, nice gray pants, and shiny black shoes, apologized that he couldn't get us a ride but promised to drop us at a place that welcomed hitchhikers. That sounded just a bit odd, like "why would a town welcome hitchhikers?" But he went on and on about how we should walk into town, that this was a very welcoming place, etc.

What could we say, other than "okay…"

He pulled over at the exit. We hopped out, and he had to open the trunk very carefully as the wire to the towering antenna would disconnect if he opened it too much. I managed to squeeze my rucksack out but noticed that a side pocket on it was partly opened. I asked him to let me take a look, but he explained about the antenna and shut the trunk lid. I found later than my folding knife had slipped out which, considering our circumstances, was a terrible loss.

We walked into the little Idaho town, trying to catch rides and, still believing our driver, expecting to get picked up. No rides were forthcoming, despite brisk traffic. We finally settled down to just walking and entered the tiny suburban area. Passing a man working in his front yard, Mike loudly called "hello, sir!" as was his custom. Oddly, the man straightened up and silently stared at us for a full minute as we walked past, with us staring back.

Finding the little center of town, we discovered a bright, airy café that doubled as the town bar. It was nearly empty, so we chose a table, dropped our packs, and sat down. It was the kind of place that we expected table service, and although there was a couple of staff on duty, none ventured forth. Mike went up to the bar and got us a couple of mugs of coffee. When hungry, you pour all kinds of things into your coffee for sustenance, and we occupied ourselves with this for some time.

At last we noticed that, still, no one was interested in waiting on us, so we both went up to the bar to chat. We had a little patter that we'd developed over the days, which we began by asking the bartender where we might camp for the night. The bartender, casting a cold, odd eye on us, asked, "Did you boys hitchhike in here?"

"Yessir," still smiling.

"You didn't get a ride, did you?"

My forearms began to feel cold, and I straightened up.

"No, sir."

"Well, you ain't gonna get a ride *out* of here, neither."

I stepped back from the bar, as if he'd pulled a knife.

"In fact, you'll be lucky to get out of here at all."

I was stunned, my mouth open, unable to comprehend what the man was saying. I instinctively dropped back toward the packs, unsure of what danger there was nor from what corner it might come.

Mike remained firmly at the bar. I could tell he was off-balance, but to anyone else, he would've looked calm. He actually managed another smile for the bartender and asked him, in so many words, "What do you mean?"

Turns out a well-liked local woman had picked up a hitchhiker just the week prior. He had raped and murdered the woman, stolen her car, and dumped her body across the line in Washington State. The entire community was enraged and grieving.

Our traveling salesman had a wicked sense of humor.

We managed to warm our frosty host just a bit, and he acquiesced to selling us a sandwich, which we split between us as the day's meal. Grateful that the bartender no longer shot hate toward us, we sipped coffee and discussed, in low tones, our next move.

Thanking our host, who was able to muster a nod, we shouldered our loads and headed back down the little road we had come in on, cussing and discussing our earlier driver and walking fast. The little community had become aware of our presence, and although we no longer turned around to try to hitch rides, some of the local boys took pleasure in pitching beer cans at us. One pickup turned around repeatedly to roll by, the passenger casting anything at hand at us on the way by. We weren't hit by anything solid, but plenty of liquids spilled across us during the melee. The pickups approaching from the rear would suddenly begin making the crunching sound of swerving off the road and onto the shoulder, and so in our haste, we repeatedly had to jump back-and-forth across the ditch to avoid the threatening vehicles. Sunset was near at hand, and there was no way I wanted to be stranded at the freeway ramp in the dark with this hornets' nest swarming 'round.

In what proved to be our best "merger" of the trip, Mike and I saw the same solution at the same time. Across from us, the roadside was dense with trees. We trudged quickly along on our side, talking to each other, but not wanting to telegraph that we were working on our plan. During a lull in the pickup traffic, we quickly scurried across the road and into the dense woods. To our delight, there was a deep flume just beyond the tree line, and we were able to crouch in that virtually unseen. We stayed there for some time, with the locals roaring back and forth, finally using their headlights in an effort to locate us. As night descended, we traversed the slope to our left, still in the belly of the flume, and eventually emerged on the flank of a broad hill, out of site of the highway and with a gorgeous view of the valley below. The night was warm, and although we didn't light a fire (so as not to draw attention), our camp felt warm and safe.

The stars that night were a wonder, and our open slope allowed for a broad view of the heavens.

In the orange dawn, we could plainly see the freeway interchange below us, and we quickly worked back to the two-lane and, walking briskly, followed it to the main artery

74

unmolested. I said a prayer for that poor woman and a curse for the traveling salesman. We quickly caught a ride west, surprisingly from someone coming from the direction of the little town... go figure. He drove us into Washington State and we left the nightmare of that crime and our punishment behind us.

Chapter Twenty-One

Ritzville

Ritzville, Washington, is a dab of color in the midst of a sea of flat, open space. Ritzville is Washington's answer to the farm burgs of the Midwest, with silos towering like high-rises and burger stands serving as social centers.

Mike and I wandered back and forth in the same path at the side of the highway, kicking pebbles and spitting as we waited for a car to whisk into the still morning air. The sun was warm and bright, the heat of the day just beginning, when we began to get restless with the solitude of the on-ramp. Down the ramp behind us, near the intersection of the on-ramp with the highway, was another couple of 'hikers sitting against the one-way sign post (in order to be seen by the traffic actually driving on the freeway) and looking very tired of it all. We had not spoken to these two, as they were in a dangerous spot for the state of Washington. The owner of the freeway gas station explained that the Highway Patrol was very tough on hitchhikers who entered the ramp far enough to be considered on the freeway right-of-way, and we relied on his information.

"If we don't get out of here by one o'clock, I say we walk through town and try the other exit," I said.

"Eddie, look, it must be five miles through town to that exit, and it's not gonna be any better than this!"

"Yeah, Mike, but we've gotta try *some*thing."

"Well, let's just try to get a ride out of here."

We'd had a refreshing morning wash in the sink of the gas station, and I had on a relatively clean T-shirt, plunged in clean running creek water and dried by hanging on the outside of my rucksack. Things were actually in pretty good shape, as we had plenty of warm weather ahead of us, had eaten the evening before, and were growing ever-nearer to our dream: the Coast Highway and some kind of truth about this life.

It was the solitude of the freeway ramp that tamped us down.

The hours ticked by. By noon we had exhausted our games of throwing pebbles into tin cans and were tired of trying to write something in the flapping wind. We had taken turns sitting on the packs, patching a worn hole in something, or writing the odd paragraph, or even reading, while the other stood looking down the highway at the empty streets of Ritzville.

Soon after this meditative boredom settled in for serious, we were awakened back to reality by the rolling menace of the State Patrol. He passed us, but it was a frightening sight when he stopped for the couple down the highway and sent them to doggedly trudge back up the ramp past us. The officer waited, then pulled a U-turn, and, driving back up the off-ramp, disappeared. After the couple had likewise disappeared over the hump of the bridge, Mike and I decided to tempt fate. We figured that the officer had just been here, probably had a huge area to cover, and that after such a mind-numbing morning, we stood a much better chance of action down nearer to the actual roadway.

No sooner had we passed through the forbidden plane of the chain-link fence than the patrolman reappeared and drove toward us over the same hump. Immediately, Mike and I turned and began walking toward legal ground, but the officer stopped and accosted us before we made it back to safety.

"Hold it right there, fellas." He seemed to smile as he called to us through the window of his cruiser, but I didn't feel any friendliness between us. He climbed out of the car and walked slowly toward us, looming high in his storm-trooper boots and Smokey-the-Bear hat. I felt buck-naked.

"You fellas *want* a ticket, don't you?" As if the principal in elementary school, he waited patiently for one of us children to squeak out an answer.

"No, sir."

"Well, why the hell are you heading over there, after I just got done talking to those other folks?" I felt sick over this cat-and-mouse game and looked at the man without answering.

"Well, I'll tell ya, fellas, I could haul you in now and be done with it, *or* I can give you a warning. What'll it be?" Again, he waited like an elderly schoolmarm for her delinquent boys to come up with an answer.

Mike did answer: "Well, we'd rather just have a warning sir... uhhh... where is it that we should stand?" Although I was a bit jaded from being through this many times before, Mike has an innocent face, and he spoke as if the cop might actually give us a break just based on that.

"You see that fence there?" We had fallen just three feet short of it in our scurry back up the ramp. "Well, if you just stand a few good strides the other side of that, no one will bother you. Okay?"

"Sure, sure, sounds good." Mikey was beaming.

"Good." Slight pause. "Now let's see some IDs."

I felt a familiar stab of anxiety, as if I were on the run from the law, and briefly considered desperate action. As I dug in a side pocket of my bag, I reviewed the past few months: nothing more heinous than pot and beer. I began to settle down.

"Just wait right here for a minute, boys, and I'll run a quick check." As he strolled back toward the patrol car, an auto passed heading in our direction, and I winced at the loss of having missed a possible ride. The situation at hand called for prudence. The auto slipped from my mind as it slipped from my vision.

We watched carefully as the officer called in our names and license numbers. He then sat quietly, eyeing us over, waiting for a report. Finally, the word came over in a crackling voice that we were not wanted. The patrolman smiled, took the time to write out our warnings, and then carefully re-crossed the pavement to give us our cards.

"So, you're from Ohio, huh?"

I smiled. "Yeah, up near Cleveland."

"No kidding. I've got a sister that's living outside of Cleveland. Bay Village I think." Mike told me later that a crack about the guy's sister flashed across his mind, but he managed to stifle himself.

We were playing on his good humor. "Yeah, yeah, sure I've got some friends in Bay Village. What's her name?" I asked.

"Dillow, Georgia Dillow. I think the name of the street is Lake Overlook or something like that." I told Mike later that *I* had a crack about the guy's sister flash across *my* mind at that moment, but I simply smiled and stared. We feigned serious thought for a moment, searching our memories for someone we'd never met, in a town we'd never been to. I couldn't think of a single person I knew in Bay Village.

"No, no, I can't think of anybody by that name…"

"Well, there's a lot of people in Cleveland."

"Yeah…" We were smiling and ending the conversation. The patrolman turned and moved toward his car as we picked up our loads and headed back beyond the fence to safer ground.

Chapter Twenty-Two

The Specter of Responsibility

Following the conversation with Officer Phillips of the Washington State Patrol, we walked back up the on-ramp, constantly rehashing the conversation with the officer, adding garnishes here and there, and sorting out exactly what we should have said. His sister's married name of Dillow was just too good, and we pummeled that word gag for thirty minutes. Finally, with the humor waning and feeling relaxed and relieved, Mike left his bag and ran over the hump of the bridge to check on the other two hitchhikers.

They were gone.

"Eddie, dammit, those people got a ride already!" He was jubilant and angry, but my first reaction was fear that maybe the cop had taken them in. "Well, I don't know, Mike."

"Let's check that map." We carefully unfolded the battered paper map of the area and studied it silently for several minutes.

"Look, Eddie, I'm tired of this fucking Washington. Let's head to Oregon and get out of this town."

I looked down the road from where it began over our little bridge to where it disappeared around a small bluff in the distance. When Michael and I had first arrived, there was a lone 'hiker there, so at least one if not both parties had escaped via this southern route.

"Well... umm... okay, Mike, if you think it's the best way to go."

"It'll probably be a little warmer down there anyway; let's get going." He was already reloading his amusements, a pad, a pen, and a paperback book, into his bag.

I was not convinced of this business of it being warmer a little bit south of here, and besides, the day was ablaze around us. It was the night, of course, to which he referred.

I was as burned out on this tiny burg as a boy away from home could be, so I followed Mikey, a little less jubilant than he was, across the bridge and onto the asphalt road heading south.

Dan picked us up almost immediately. His small son Joshua was neither happy nor impressed with our intrusion into the cab of the pickup. We, on the other hand, were ecstatic to get a ride and to find this beautiful small bundle in the front of an ancient Chevy. We bellowed south on the highway, Dan smiling, telling us that his nickname was "Moe" ("Mohrmann" as I later learned) and telling us stories, while we all got high and giggled with little Josh.

Moe led us south from our troubled past in Ritzville to the Tri-Cities area: Kennewick, Pasco, and Richland, Washington. As we wound south, so the day wound down, pleasant and relaxed, with the landscape turning to an absolute desert as we neared the Tri-Cities area. Moe was helping to build a power plant.

The evening passed easily in Dan's front room, and he proved to be as generous as anyone I've ever met. The food and beer flowed as freely from his refrigerator as did laughter from his lips. We washed our clothes in his machine, chatted with the people next door, and generally began to feel at home. Moe lent me his truck, and I drove to the corner store for more beer and rolling papers. All was heavenly.

We in turn invaded Dan's bare bathroom, and the grime washed out of our pores as if we'd been to the beach that day. Accumulated grit and sand, behind our ears, in our noses, between our toes, loosened with difficulty but eventually fell away into the drain of the tiny shower stall. I emerged as fresh and bright as when I crossed the Minnesota border.

As adolescents, Mike and I found ourselves between older Dan and younger Josh. I'm a poor judge of age, but I guess Moe was thirty or so. I constantly found myself with one foot in his adult world and one foot in Josh's child-world. As the company was easy-going, I delighted in both.

That evening found us in conversation with a couple in the trailer just down the dirt road from Moe, and it appeared that they, as everyone in this camp, were connected to the power plant construction in some way or another. The man of that house was an ex-con and an electrician.

"Yeah, Billy done some time a couple of years ago, but he's all over that now, ain't ya Billy?" The lady of the house was talking nonstop, full of news, but I could hear a touch of fear and uncertainty in her voice. Billy looked slowly around the room, smiling a hard line at us, mocking with his eyes.

"Yeah, sure, I'm all through with that shit." He gave a small laugh. "Sure."

"Well, hey, who's for gettin' high?" Dan seemed to have an unlimited capacity for marijuana, and I simply could not keep up. He continually surprised me, as his activities veered between focus on son Josh and fervency for getting loaded. I was fooled now, as Moe reacted to my decline of his offer in a kind and comfortable tone. "A little too toasted, huh?" He was fatherly to me in caring for my state of mind. "Never mind, man, we'll do a little more later."

The evening rose and crashed in waves of altered consciousness, and when we were in a lucid interval, Mike and I spent some time in deliberation and decided (at Moe's suggestion) to stay on at his place for another day. We ended the evening pleasantly, with me trailing off to the child's room to sleep on the floor. The heat of the day and the seductions of the night had dragged both Michael and me into oblivion. I fell into my bag, with a great heave of relief, and dreamt wildly of lands unseen and before us.

I awoke in the morning, with the light streaming in the window and the child Joshua gone. I crawled about, gathering my clothes and puzzling out where I was. I delighted to hear Michael's voice harmonizing with the barely audible stereo and to smell food cooking. I hurried out.

"Sit down, Eddie, have some coffee; I'll have chow ready in a minute." Mike was in a wonderful mood, a reflection of our host's generosity, and was nearly finished preparing eggs, bacon, and toast. We ate in relaxed, expectant ease.

"This guy is really something, Mikey. Letting us have his house for the day, giving us his food, his beer,"

Mike was chomping down a huge mouthful of eggs and toast, but responded right through them. "Yeah!" He sounded muffled. "I wish there was something we could do."

I looked around the place, trying to find some chore that would be appropriate. None availed itself. "I don't know man, there's not much to do in here, and Josh's room looks pretty good."

"Yeah, I know, but maybe we'll find something."

From the kitchen table, we moved out through a utility cubicle to the back steps of the trailer and sipped coffee in the morning sun. The air was still quite cool, but the rising sun kept off the chill. We spotted Billy's woman flopping down the street in her clogs.

"Liz! Liz! Yeah, it's us! C'mon over!" Liz seemed hesitant and I thought that maybe she couldn't see too well, as she didn't turn toward us until Michael called again.

"Hi. Uuuhhhh... how are you guys this morning?" Liz was hesitant with us, and I now suspected that sex was central in her life, and that *nothing* should come between her and Billy. I smiled an innocent smile and tried to relieve her. We were not pursuing her.

"Liz, are you hung-over this morning?" My question was just a little too flat, and it drew some attention to itself. She remained stiff with us.

"No." Pause. "No, uh-uh. How about you?"

"Well, a little, but Michael here has cooked up a good breakfast, so I feel all right."

"And Budwin ate it all!"

"Oh, that's funny..." Liz looked from me to Mike and then to me again. "I didn't know your name was Budwin!"

We shared a small laugh, and Mike explained that my name was really Eddie. Liz was not overly interested in the entire matter. "Look, Liz, what we really want to know is if there's anything we can do for Moe to sort of make up for all that he's been doing for us. Can you think of anything?" Liz's eyes lit up a little and she suddenly seemed much more relaxed. I sensed that she was vulnerable and innocent beyond the hardness of her Billy. Liz sat down and began to babble about her good friend Danny, and I could see the joy rise in her eyes as she spoke.

"Well look, man, if Danny wanted anything from you, he'd of said so. He doesn't want anything, man. Just to help people out when he can. He just wants to give you a hand, and maybe you'll help somebody else, and then maybe that guy'll help somebody else, see?" She spoke in a tone of amazement and was out of breath when she finished.

"So, y'see, when Danny helps you, don't try to offer him anything or get uptight about it, man; just flow with it, y'know? Just be sure to help somebody else out when they need it, okay?"

"Sure, Liz, sure, that's really great." Mike and I were grinning big, and really enjoying this idea, and also growing a little tired of Liz's constant chatter.

"Where you headed, Liz?" I asked.

"Oh, I was just headin' up to the store for some eggs and stuff. Do you want to come along?" She was brimming with sister-and-brotherhood now, but Mike and I were up for a quiet morning and made an excuse.

"Well, thanks, Liz, but we've got to get our tent set up and dried out. Can't let it get moldy, y'know."

"Okay, I gotta get going, but don't worry about Danny, man, he doesn't expect anything."

Mike and I turned inside and rinsed out our cups. We walked slowly through the trailer and decided on a few things to do.

"I've gotta keep the tent dry, Mike."

"Ah, Eddie, it won't rot in one *day*. You been takin' good care of it."

"But it's borrowed; it wouldn't be right to neglect it."

He got to work inside, and I rolled out the tent, which was still sopping wet from two days ago, making me feel a little guilty about getting so high the night before. I draped it over Josh's tiny swing set in the postage-stamp backyard and immediately saw the moisture drying in the sun. All looked fine.

Back inside, Michael was washing the dishes, which we had collected from all parts of the trailer.

"Whaddya make of Dan?" I was now straightening up the front room while Mikey dried the dishes.

"I dunno, Ed. I can't believe he's got a kid and still does all the shit he does."

"Yeah, I can't *believe* the way he smokes pot. Wow!"

"How *old* do you think he is?"

"I don't know that either. I mean, he acts so crazy, but he must be thirty or something."

"Naw, Ed, he's not that old, maybe twenty-five or so."

The question was answered later that day when Dan's babysitter brought Josh back home. Mike and I were pleasantly stoned in the front room, listening to a couple of albums and folding our cleaned-and-dried clothes for the packs. I was surprised to have her walk in without knocking and jumped up to face the door.

"Oh! Ah… well… excuse me… are you guys friends of Dan's?" She blushed red.

"Sort of… we were hitchhiking yesterday and he picked us up and brought us here."

"Oh, okay… sure… he told me about you guys, but he couldn't think if you were staying or not."

I looked at Mikey and we smiled. Dan's generosity had been our favorite topic of the day, but his faith that we wouldn't steal his stuff and leave was very sweet. He seemed a spaced-out disciple of good.

When Peggy Anne had settled in a bit, we pressed her for information.

"Yeah, well, Dan was married, and his old lady took off to live in a tipi in Idaho. Dan was really hurt by all that, and he had to go up there and take Josh away…" and she went on like that for quite a while, filling us in on the tragedy and the mirth of Dan.

After some time, I said, "Whew, sounds like he's had a hard time of it."

"Yeah, but he's such a nice guy." I had been suspicious for a while, but her intonation on the "such a nice guy" confirmed it. The babysitter was in love with the daddy. She couldn't have been twenty years old.

"So how old *is* he, anyway?"

"Well, he's a little older than me [this to let us know about the relationship], and he's been working at the plant for five years now, so I think he's about twenty-six."

I got up from the floor to get another beer and thought about things for a while. When Mike and I had a moment in the kitchen, we spoke alone.

"He's got one foot with the kid and one with Peggy." Mike thought this was delightful and expressed that Dan was doing a great job of holding off that inevitable American Dream with which we are all confronted.

"Yeah, well, I think it's great, *too*, man, but how long can he keep that up?"

We soon found out.

When Dan came home, he was embarrassed and pleased with the little chores we had done around the trailer. He thanked us repeatedly and had us sit down to smoke his favorite pipe with him. He was delighted, it appeared, to have two such noble guests in his home. *We* became embarrassed, eventually, of the hubbub he made every time he stepped into another room. Peggy Anne became just as pleased, hanging on his arm to caress him with each new crest of silliness. Things became clearer to me as we spoke.

"It's a real pleasure to have you guys here. This is great. We won't have to clean for a month, will we, Josh?" Josh stared at him unintelligibly, his diapered bottom teetering on two shaky legs.

As the evening wore on, Dan's appreciation of us grew, as did the one-sided love affair of Peggy Anne. She clung to Dan as he moved about, he carrying on a stoned monologue and touching Peggy's face now and then to affirm her presence.

Billy and Liz stomped in, this time featuring Liz as our new pal, and Dan gave them the embarrassment tour, all full of exclamations and stoned laughter. Liz loved her new, hard-working brothers.

A carbon-copy of the night before began to unfold, the pot and beer flowing. It became a sad distraction to the others when we slowly revealed that we planned to move on in the morning.

Billy, in his reserved and hungry manner, didn't comment on our plans. He was the only one of the group who did not insist that we stay for at least another day. But the signals were all very clear. Dan's attachment to us, total strangers, and Liz's admiration for us, simple raggedy travelers, told us that we needed to keep moving.

Somehow, despite the relative affluence of the adults in the room, and despite the security of their very good jobs, it gradually emerged that they were envious of our adventure. We simply hadn't expected that.

The night wound to a close with all of us too high and drunk to really say goodbye, but we had several periods of strained conversation concerning our leaving before everyone mercifully let us be. I grew impatient and upset each time the group tried to talk us into staying long-term, for the reasons, including the good jobs at the plant, were all wrong. Dan's plight with his young woman and his son, and his admiration of our simple travels, became more embarrassing than fun. Everyone's struggle to escape their particular role was a growing burden to us, as they looked to us to pull them along. All except for Billy: he remained within at all times, locked in a self-designed cell, never wishing to emerge.

"I wish these people didn't feel this way about us," I whispered to Mike as we curled up in the darkness. "It's like *they* need *us* or something."

"Well, Eddie, it just looks like they never had the chance, man. It'll be better in the morning."

In the morning it *was* better, with Moe waking us with the sounds of cooking and the dawn still very fresh and unreal outside the trailer. Dan wore a big smile as we stumbled out and began to stuff our belongings into our bags. At first I glanced at him carefully, but he was genuinely happy in the golden light, and we were delighted to speak heartily with him over hot eggs.

"It's been really great having you guys here. A real pleasure. Sorry about last night, but y'know, we hate to see you leave so soon."

"It's been really great *being* here, Dan, " I said. "I can't believe how good it's been. It's just that we have to keep movin', man. Got a lot of ground to cover."

We talked openly, and as we all got ready, Dan's woman Peggy sleepily made her way out to wish us goodbye. I was surprised to see her standing in the bedroom door, trying to wake up, child-like and frail. I suddenly felt a deep attachment to her, and although I was younger than she, I felt the urge to protect and care for her.

Packed and ready to go, we presented Peggy Anne with our wide-awake faces and loud goodbyes. She leaned forward, held the back of my neck in her warm hand, and pecked me on the cheek.

Her breath was terrible.

"So long, man," she was barely audible. "Take care of yourself."

"You take care of our Dan, now, hear?" I whispered, her face close to mine. I felt the warmth of her hand on my neck for months afterward.

Mike in turn received his kiss, and then we headed outside into the clear morning sun, listening for that highway song.

Moe popped out a minute later, his face beaming maybe a little too much, and we piled into his ancient cab. We rolled quietly out of the trailer park and then hit the boulevard hard, heading into the sun for a mile or so to the main artery. Dan turned south in our direction, but was not sure where to stop. Mike and I soon discerned the problem, that he had never been a hitchhiker, and asked Dan to drop us off at the next crossroads.

"Well, look, there should be a better place than *that* around here." We all knew, of course, that there wouldn't really be a better place, and so he agreed to pull over. The crossroad was a tiny one: a thin scar over the flat land.

"Well, take it easy, you guys."

"Yeah, Dan, we will. We've got your address, man, so we'll send you a letter. Take care." I slammed the door a little too soon, as Dan was still looking at us, but as he wheeled around, his grinning face was framed in the open driver's window. We could all feel the connection between us as he wound her up through the gears.

As the pickup disappeared down the highway, heading north, I felt something give in me. I tasted something metallic in my mouth, and I wished that we could have Dan back with us for a moment. But I also knew at that moment that I had grown up, and that my tie with Dan was broken, as it was with so many things as we fought our way west. I thought back on Minnesota, where I felt so fresh and young, and of Cleveland, which I could barely remember, and of the many people I'd met since then.

I knew then that my tie with Danny was broken, and I stared down the highway after his truck.

I wrote a letter to Moe many months later, but it came back unopened. He had moved on, without leaving a forwarding address, with his young assistant, Joshua.

Chapter Twenty-Three

Green Apples

It was in southwest Washington State and then in northeast Oregon ("Ory-gun") that we began to feel alive and free in ourselves. Without really meaning to, we worked our way over to the head of the Columbia Gorge and then west on the Columbia River Highway. The land and the people were unassuming and to some extent uncaring about our actions, and the independence was refreshing. After many days on the road, with the constant need of help to get us out of the cold and rain, we found ourselves in warmer weather, and we became less active in pursuing the rides for which we once worked so diligently. Following an easy evening ride, our driver suggested that we head south down a dirt road, and sure enough, we found a wonderful place to camp for the night.

It was a good place. Really, a very fine place. The high grasses were a cushion for, and the low-hung apple branches a cover for, our tiny tent; and it was doubtful that anyone, much less the cops, would try to make it down the bumpy dirt road leading to this place. It even had a pond nearby, with the singing of the highway just near enough to hear.

Perhaps it was the apples, small green apples hanging bunched from the old trees surrounding the tent, that made this place memorable. We smeared the last of our food, dabs of peanut butter, on the apples as we ate them, filling ourselves on the salt-sour-crunch taste and giving praise to the sunset with our eyes and mouths.

I'm not sure if it was the apples that made a change in me, but I remember them most clearly now. It was the end of the food and the end of the money at the end of an abandoned road, two thousand miles from Cleveland, Ohio.

Maybe it was the green apples, for a lesson seemed to grow from them. It sprang from them, as they marked the end of protection, of safety. We had given most of our protection away long ago, and now we had eaten the last of it.

We wondered how to go forward, and during our conversation I was a bit shaken. The sunset answered us as we spoke, asking us not to waver now that our protection was gone, for it was our unwavering faith in the sun which had allowed our protection to work.

The lesson was explained by the darkness, as Mike and I were slowly surrounded by it.

We believed we had protection because we had food and money, but those actually made us vulnerable. The chance that we might lose the money or the food left us open to despair. But now we were at zero. We owned almost nothing, had nothing to lose. Now, at last, we were free and had real protection, for only good could come to us. Evil had been eliminated. By not having, we could not lose, and therefore all to occur will be but guidance to us. Just as surely as faith in dawn would carry us through the night, so also our belief that good will come to us for our needs.

Yes, I'm quite sure it was the apples, brilliant white beneath florescent green skins. I crunched as I strolled down the dirt road, tent on my back and Mike in front of me, full of faith in the morning.

Chapter Twenty-Four
End of the Quest

Reaching the Pacific Ocean, which was of such importance to me, was a much quieter affair than I had imagined. After sunset, a ride took us to the Coast Highway, and the driver, a little surprised by my request, pointed the way down a little tarmac road which ended at the beach.

Lugging my rucksack with me, leaving my heavy shoes on, I strode purposefully westward, the waves a light hiss in the gloaming, and walked directly into the sea. I was speechless. We had made it. The poontang-rich smell, the cool wet on my feet, the light breeze in my hair.

I wept.

Mike hung back on the beach, shaking his head that I was risking my shoes. He was happy and amused but not as swept away as I, which was a bit strange since he always loved the ocean, pronouncing it *"The Ocean!"* ever since he had discovered it at a dirty New Jersey beach many years prior. Columbus would have been envious of the celebration of Mike's first day at the beach, but not this day.

I stood for longer than I should've, allowing my feet to get completely soaked, and then turning to the mundane chores at hand, walked back to the road and the lights.

We were starving but could find no food, so trawled instead for a safe, secret place to sleep.

The important thing was: we had made it!

Chapter Twenty-Five
The Long and the Short of It

We reached the West Coast, and the possibility of some work, just in time. Mike was usually the first one up and out of the tent in the morning, a lover of sunrises. But after our first night camping on the Oregon coast, I was up and sipping hot water for some time before he crawled out of the mouth of the little tent. His shock of blond hair was an unusually messy affair that morning, and he was dead silent. He walked slowly over to where I was sitting on a log and, with a grimace, sat down and sipped on the cup of steaming water I offered.

When he finally turned to look at me, I was alarmed. His eyes were glassy and unfocused. He tried to manage a smile, but it came out more like a grimace.

"What's going on, Mike?"

His voice was a little raspy: "I feel like my stomach is eating itself."

"Did you try that trick with your knuckles?"

He turned on me, almost in a rage: "A course I tried the trick! I tried everything I can think of!"

He was really not himself. Hunger had finally turned on him, and he was shaky and unsteady when he stood up to take a leak.

Then I remembered I had a package of dry noodle soup that I was keeping in deep reserve, a "just-in-case" packet of food which I'd thought I might keep *always* in reserve, but I was frightened by the depth of Michael's hunger. I immediately dug the battered package out of the bottom of my bag and, after adding more water to our little pot, got 'er boiling again and added the noodles. I felt elated that I had something to offer him but somewhat concerned that this was indeed the very last of our food. I was still learning the lesson from the green apples.

Chapter Twenty-Six

Children

How I happened to end up on the Oregon coast with Mike, of all people, is a good question. The fact that I was in Oregon was not all that surprising; I had been planning this trip for nine months. But I was just getting to know this guy, and I had originally planned a solo trip.

The fact that we were on the coast was inalterable, but how we got there, and what has transpired since, seems to ripen and sweeten with age. It has been the same for so many things along the road.

To begin with, we were on the coast, many miles from Cleveland, Ohio, and I wasn't sure that I even liked the guy, not to mention the fact that we slept together every night and went without showering for days. "How the hell did I end up *here*?" I'd been mumbling every evening, for several evenings, when I crawled into my sleeping bag, Mike having previously racked, with his smelly shoes in the mouth of the tiny tent.

Most assuredly, we were on the coast, as the cool mist of the early morning cleansed our bodies of the night's sleep, even though we were high on a coastal wall, overlooking the pounding surf and drinking the air from the Oriental current below.

Most assuredly, we were on the coast, for the ocean was full and deep in our faces, and the awe of the permanence of the thing filled us each day; the unending repetition of the cleansing waves, scrubbing against the wall of America; the roaring vicissitudes of eastward flow, patiently grinding against the rough hide of our country.

After Mike got some food in him, he was elated at rediscovering *"The Ocean!"* Ever after, Mike the Explorer expounded upon his discovery of the Pacific, to publicize the gravity of his find, gladly doing so at the slightest mention of any watery subject. This began to grow as ripe with age as our boots.

The Coast Highway through Oregon is a rainy, rugged affair, with the rocks of the coast jutting into the water at hard angles, making little peninsulas. We traveled slowly through this area, the locals giving us short lifts and the tourists eyeballing us through green-tinted glass as they swam by. Mike and I were full of the life of the coast, with me leaving dread and fear behind me as we worked south. I was slowly recovering from the troubles at home and feeling better about the prospects ahead. We had a little money in our pockets from day labor, including a half-day of unloading lumber, which provided both food and cash. The prospects of warmer weather down the line cheered me.

The last ride had dropped us here on the coast of Oregon by a matter of choice. The driver, a veritable bear of a man, was headed to Yachats. He was a burly, self-reliant guy with a volcanic outer appearance, who practiced a sensitive trade. He was a spinning-wheel maker, and Yachats held a community of skilled craftsmen, all bent on overcoming the junk craft markets along the coast road. I so admired his descriptions of the craftsmen, dedicated to their trades along this tourist-infested highway. After a nice, medium-length ride, our driver showed Mike and me where to go through the thick curtain of green in order to reach the cliff above the perpetual sea. The hissing of receding waves led us to a tiny camp on a small finger of land which we occupied beyond the reach of man and law. Here we stayed for days. Outside the limits of electricity and engines, we spent our time in meditative quiet. A book each, a little sketching, some long walks, and a few explorations down near the waterline (where shallow caves peered up between the shrugs of waves) were more than sufficient to fill the days. Sometimes it seemed that there wasn't enough daylight when we needed the sun most. Other times, the sun was too tardy in setting, when we waited eagerly for the sky-show of stars and planets.

We relaxed and recuperated from our cold and grueling trip west. We played and dawdled and delighted in the smallest pleasures. We bickered and then immediately made up. All was remembered, and all forgotten. We found a little work and ate enough to keep us in this world.

The essence was always the same there on the coast. The breeze of the Orient passed lightly over our bodies; the books leafed effortlessly through our fingers: *Free Knowledge*! I was rereading *On the Road*, a book Mike had given me. Purity of thought descended on us as the solemnity of our wave-washed peninsula gave wing to our minds.

But of course, we were always hungry.

When one ponders food, and one is also attempting to live freely on the Oregon coast, certain variables arise which need to be taken note of.

The breezes from *"The Ocean!"* across our spit of land at once felt relieving and filling. The nutritious Japanese Current wafted through all our senses, and it seemed almost sufficient to support us physically. However, our stomachs soon brought us to realize the neglect we'd endured on the road thus far, and therefore, we had to ponder alternative nutrition.

I was actually a bit chubby when I'd struck out on this journey, and although I felt able to live on my body fat for several days should the need arise, I was wholly unable to supply a like service for my partner in the venture, as Mike was rail-thin.

Consider for a moment a six-foot, two-inch lad in his late teens, healthfully slim, and capable of devouring enormous mounds of food at any one sitting. Remove this lad, if you will, from the comforts of the living room in which you now find yourself, and transport him to a remote stretch of beach fifteen hundred miles from his home. Now remove all funds and foodstuffs from his pockets, and examine the end product: this is a forlorn sight.

Modern science has, at least in part, addressed this quandary. Indeed, although the verdant green of the coastline provided the air, sea, peace, and serenity of these children's garden, it was our rucksacks which provided for the physical, chiefly in the form of inexpensive, dried soups. Combined with the occasional bit of meat and complimented by local fruit or produce, these foodstuffs were capable of filling (even at times filling *enough*) the bottomless chasm of Mike's stomach.

You may be wondering, following the long-winded description above, just what the coast actually provides. Already related are the unending waves and ocean breezes, which perpetually sweep the land near the shore. Above this, there is a great abundance of fruit and vegetables grown in the region, to be had (legally!) for a miniscule price.

Two other very natural resources, however, make the Oregon coast one of the most hospitable areas in our wide country. These are the milk of human kindness, which seems to flow from every crevice in the inhabited areas west of the Cascades, and firewood, the like and abundance of which remains unmatched.

To consider the tenderer of these two virtues, one need only to lay himself at the mercy of the fates in this region, that is, the entire coastal range of our thirty-third state. Let one be vulnerable, say in the case of Mike and me, and invariably the answer is found in others. Consider the aforementioned spinning-wheel maker: that good man provided us an afternoon of labor in exchange for good company, an eight-pack of beer, and a few dollars, which we immediately spent on locally-grown foods. The milk of kindness and the produce contributed to our general well-being, but also to Mike's rather depleted reserves.

Again, allow one to enter the local food emporium for even the briefest of moments… undoubtedly a long conversation will begin, involving not only the weather and the vegetables, but also one's present disposition. It's as if the constant warm pulsations of the nearby surf have lulled the locals to insensitivity to the coldness of mankind, and the barriers common to the rest of us are washed away like so much sea-sand before the relentless waves. Of course the weather does get cold and wet there, but the inner glow of the people provides constant warmth.

The second virtue, firewood, is of an entirely different nature. The consuming aspect of the subject makes a lasting example difficult to present, yet the evidence is overwhelming, that the driftwood on the Oregon coast is of the best quality to be had.

Being from the Midwest, I've often known firewood to be damp and deciduous. On the coast, the beach is thickly bearded with wood, which is, though provided by the sea, a wondrous light, dry, and nearly spontaneously-combustible heat source. The color: a soft gray hue which evinces the very essence of gentleness and power. But it is the burn which is the key, the finest for brewing coffee and cooking food. The camp chow was continuously blessed with the smell, taste, and essence of this refreshing smoke. The sea provides, and the wood cast upon the Oregon shore emanates the beautiful Oriental current to those who would receive.

We were able to survive two days and a morning on each round of "bought" food, although only as much as our meager funds would allow. We were bodily cared for, and our minds and spirits soared with the morning and evening breezes.

We reveled in our freedom, and it's important to note that the means of attaining this freedom are not for every man. The comfort and love of the open air which we enjoyed are not the "bread and butter" of the next man. Its purchase price includes sleeping on the ground night after night, with a thin wall of tent between one and the elements. But this point is relative: to one who perceives physical comforts as an extension of one's self, this humble life would be unacceptable; to the next man, the discomfort of sleeping on the ground is a blessing. To me, the situation was utopia: modern science provided me with a tiny, portable house, which kept us and our gear dry, and food to which I might add two cups of water, then boil and eat. This was not first class on the traveler's train, but quite sufficient for our contentment and happiness.

So our bodies were supplied with necessities, and our souls filled with the lovely breezes, colorful sunsets, and fragrant smoke of our little stretch of coastline. Our days rocked gently by with the firm repetition of the waves, and we were lulled to sleep.

Which brings me back to the original question of this chapter: what was I doing on the Oregon coast, with a "crazy" man? By circuitous route, we have arrived at the approximation of an answer: to think. And to think properly, one must be secure in body and mind. Our basic needs filled, we found ourselves at the very best place to exercise our freedom: the pulsating shoreline of the Pacific.

Lulled to sleep, and yet speeding onward with all of our minds, our thoughts ran smoothly and rapidly through the portals and crevices of our upbringing. Sleeping, and yet wide awake, our bodies were caressed into security, stroked to contentment by the surf. Dreaming, and vivid of thought, our minds were lifted and colored by the fresh gusts off the ocean current. Lulled to bodily serenity by the ocean, and then cast speeding, ethereally, by the flying scud of wave-crests.

Truly then, the answer is obvious to me as I write even now. We traveled, and forsaking our comfort and the security of home, denying ourselves the privilege of convention, and forfeiting the love of those we held dear, we drank at the breast of the all-nourishing Pacific to revitalize the strength of our souls and minds at the natural spring of life eternal, the ever-wandering, omnipotent current of *"The Ocean!"*

Chapter Twenty-Seven

Below Yachats

It seemed late by the time we were awake, the day we decided to move southward. The green curtain to our east sheltered us from the brilliant morning sun, leaving the tent moist. We left the tent up as we prepared the morning repast: hot coffee, to get the day off right, and the easiest of morning fare, biscuits and pats of butter from the roadside café of last evening.

With the tent dry, and the sunlight strong and white, we rolled our belongings together and sipped the last of the coffee, feeling that goodness of the last butter-rich crumbs wash down with the coffee. It was just right.

It was so right that I nearly laughed as we broke through the green shield which had guarded us from the road during the night. It was a beautiful sight: the road, winding, just a short section visible to us, pretty in the morning green, the shadows and the light sharp and clear. I was at one with the road, and as we stumbled a few steps down to the tarmac, I looked down at my feet on this man-made earth and felt my feet as part of the road. There seemed no other thing in the world but our tiny domain and the frame of my feet on the pavement.

A tourist car, huge and out-of-place, the old man driving and the white-haired wife holding a map in front of her face, rolled solemnly toward us. We didn't even raise our thumbs. He gave a puff on his cigar and she dropped the map to give us a good once-over and then their cool green-tinted boat was behind us.

I looked down the road where the green yacht had just gone. There was a very small bridge nearby. I thought I could hear, and then moments later was sure I could hear, the bushes crackling fifty yards beyond our small bridge. With a smash, another dirty, be-packed hitchhiker stumbled down the matted sand to the road. He was bearded, looking exquisitely self-sufficient, and simply sat down on his filthy yellow pack, leaving the earth.

I thought of myself as something of a seasoned man of the road, but I felt adolescent compared to this holy man. He was in no hurry to move down the highway, in contrast to Mike and me who were standing and ever-eager to earn a ride. He certainly would have dismissed the old folks in the green behemoth.

Mike and I moved to the bridge, and as it had become a meditative morning, we were quite happy to hang around the end of the span, staring into the water below. Gradually, however, I began to steal glances at our filthy companion, and gradually came to stare quite openly at him. I wasn't really sure about it, and neither was he. We stared at each other over the small gorge between us, sussing each other without being aggressive. If I'd a tail, I would have twitched it, just enough to show that I was interested. I fixed my eyes without staring hard, and left myself open to scrutiny. He did the same. Mike was uninterested, seeming to be lost in his own staring contest with the creek below.

As there was no traffic to speak of, I finally walked over to talk with the man. I sat with him for some time, keeping one eye on Mikey and the northern stretch of road and one on my glossy-eyed companion. He smelled terrible, yet interesting: the usual body odor, but mixed with herbs and some kind of flower which I couldn't place. He was entirely comfortable in sitting on his pack, his back against the embankment, and shared that he would wait until we got a ride before he tried himself. He was headed home to San Francisco and shared a bit of knowledge with me. I came back to Mike with a card advertising "Free Crash Pads" and a free bookstore and news about a startling new band we should look for: The Grateful Dead. He had also given me directions to a great beach campsite near the California border. I had left my copy of *On the Road* with my meditative friend, to which Mike's outer corners of his mouth drooped down in mild surprise and disapproval.

My interactions with the smelly "holy man" only reinforced my sense that we were on the right track, that what we were looking for lay just ahead; and that secrets, more mysterious and powerful than I could imagine, were awaiting us in mythical San Francisco.

Chapter Twenty-Eight

Pirates

Of course there were bad days, too. Waking up to the grayness of those dawns, exhilarated with the cool air, feeling a bit frightened, even, by the rainy weather. Those adrenaline feelings almost always wear off by mid-day, with the sun unable to break through, and the day dragging on without much to do but hunker down and be less miserable.

It was on a rainy coast afternoon that Larry picked us up in his clean used car. My first impressions of him were filled with ambiguity, and I sensed that he was somehow not in good shape, perhaps even ill.

Mike and I had been standing in the light mist with our rain ponchos on but our rucksacks uncovered, as covering them was only a necessity in a real rain. It was looking like an all-day affair, with the sky showing not a spot of blue above the swirly-fog, and we were hunkered down for a bone-chiller.

Larry came flapping toward us in his car, with a hesitant look and a slight swerve of his vehicle. He was eyeing the two of us over carefully, trying to sift out the highwayman in each of us, and his attention was not on the road. He crossed the yellow line two hundred feet from us, slowly curved right to the shoulder, and then began again toward the middle as he neared us.

I was also calculating *him*, and deciding whether or not to run for it, when I concluded that he was interested and would not, hopefully, run us over. He had slowed considerably by the time he reached us and rolled slowly on, staring at us without blinking, until we were well behind him.

Finally, the black and white beast pulled over to the shoulder, but so far down the road that I was unsure whether or not it was for us. We hesitated.

Suddenly, the car shifted to reverse, and we began to hurry toward it. Fearing another homicidal swerve, we kept to the shoulder of the road and signaled him to stop. He did.

The driver, Larry Olson, looked pained as we dove into his interior, our sandy packs slouched in the backseat and our rain-splattered ponchos tossed over these. He turned to me, his eyes bloodshot, and half-grinned in my moist face.

"Where ya headin'?"

"South, down to California maybe."

"Well, I'm headin' that way; I'll take ya there."

I was appalled by his presumptuousness that he would "take us there." His voice, hidden in a mask of weak ineptitude, came across like an unkind father who was empowered to transport us, if he desired.

I was at once confused and delighted in the irony of things. Mike grinned at me from the backseat, with his eyes wide and eyebrows up, and then turned to settle in for the ride.

Larry was a terrible driver.

We covered a few miles and had warmed up a little, when I opened things up with the usual "Where-ya-been? Where-ya-headin'?" banter. In my roadside panic over Larry's swerving, I had failed to note the license plates.

"Just travelin' around, seein' the country."

I was a bit in doubt as to Larry's ability, and his means for accomplishing 'seein' the country,' and questioned him further.

"Well, I want to see a lot, so I just keep drivin' and when it gets dark, I just pull over someplace and sleep."

I was still a little confused and pressed him for the facts.

"Well, I just sleep in the car when I can, and every few nights I get a room or set up a tent in a campground.

I looked at the side of his face, at his glistening right eye, and began to understand. "You just sleep in your car in parking lots and stuff?"

"Yeah, and sometimes they have little rest areas, stuff like that." Larry was exploring a bit, trying to see if we slept in "rest stops and stuff like that" as well.

I changed the subject, but continued to mull what I considered the horror of Larry's ordeal. He was from the blond state of Minnesota and worked in a plant with some of Tom Bauer's friends up at Minnetonka. Yet here he was, driving hundreds of miles a day during his two-week vacation, never leaving his car, and sleeping, exhaustedly, four hours a night in grocery store parking lots. My stomach tensed at the thought of it.

Mike had happily "left" the car and was mind-tripping along the coast, which flashed briefly between the groves as we sped southward. Things grew intermittent and then gradually silent as we rolled along, with me mulling Larry, and Larry... well, it was difficult to say where Larry was, just somewhere on the Coast Highway, heading south toward California.

The rain began to give way.

Larry seemed agitated about something and, after struggling for a slew of miles, voiced his hungry opinion. The process of driving had gotten to him as it does to so many American drivers. It is so often the case that traveling in a car produces the most pronounced hunger, even though the traveler hasn't done a damn thing all day but aim the car and read a map. I was slightly sick at the thought of stopping to eat with our driver, because I had already mentally rehearsed the scene which was to occur.

Larry slowed to a crawl, made a U-turn, and pulled into a small hamburger joint. I was pleased that he pulled into a parking spot, as this meant he would go inside instead of getting the curb-service, and this would leave Mike and me a little time to stretch and maybe walk around a little.

Mike was on the same wavelength, knowing that Larry was not about to feed a couple of freeloaders like us.

"Ain't you guys coming in?"

"Naw... naw, we'll just wait out here."

Larry hesitated for a moment and then realized we weren't going to eat. He stepped back and locked the car and, nodding to our fund-less plight, turned and walked into the diner. I was relieved.

"Whew-weee... can you imagine that guy's trip?" Mike said.

"Man, and now he's in there eating that shit at eleven in the morning!"

"Look, Bud, let's take a walk and maybe pick up a little chow." I was happy when Mike volunteered to go into the burger joint and tell Larry of our plans. We left the parking lot in a hurry.

"He doesn't want us to hold him up." Mike was quite serious as he said this, and I barked a sinister guffaw at the thought.

"What'll he be late for, his rest stop?" I was serious, too, and then thought of Larry leaving with all our gear or, perhaps worse, leaving it in the parking lot for the local hyenas to scavenge. However, I found faith in our driver's Minnesotan upbringing, and I had seen a little grocery just down the road. We hustled to the low building.

When we arrived back with a brown sack holding our dry soup, cream cheese, and crackers, Larry was leaning on the fender, working a toothpick and staring at the still-cloudy sky. He glanced at us accusingly.

"Sorry, Larry, they really take their time in there."

"Yeah, well... okay... it's okay, let's get goin'."

When our driver turned to climb in, I turned my most childish grin toward Mike, all teeth, my eyes wide. We barely stifled our laughter and piled in for much more of the same.

Larry was a dull guy who imagined that he had control of his life. I was amazed at the fallacies he told both himself and us. We had some real chokers as we rolled south. Larry's car, for instance, had been purchased at an auction of repossessed things. He had paid an outlandishly high price for his used auto, and yet he spoke of this abuse clearly and proudly, much to Mike's and my delight. It was high farce. But the final, painful irony came as we passed through a larger town.

Larry was looking for something in particular, I don't know what, and he made a sudden U-turn on the busy highway. I didn't trust Larry's driving, but at the same time I didn't feel comfortable telling him how to do it. I just braced myself.

The utility pole, much too close to the curb to begin with, had escaped Larry's notice (along with about three-quarters of the real world). A solid bugger, it was in no mood to suffer Larry's car. As our driver looked over his left shoulder at the vehicles he had just missed, the pole loomed large in my face, and I slammed my hands on the dashboard, speechless.

What a noise.

We were okay, of course, and the worst problem was Larry's bruised image of both himself and his car. I felt sorry for the guy and really felt bad about how we had abused him behind his back, yet the creased and crumpled fender only added to the urgency for us to get away from this sad child of the North and sail away on our own. I knew already that the occasion would be a touchy one.

After he ran his errand (for which we had U-turned), the farce continued in a slow, nauseating tempo, as we wound our way along the coast toward California. Mike and I were too tickled with the long, warm ride to let it go, despite our unease with our driver.

Slowly and carefully, I let my mind loose as we whirred down the highway, letting my thoughts run freely and yet carefully, so necessary when the day is long and full of drizzle. I joined Mike's mind outside the auto, and I saw the car as it moved down the road: the fender crumpled and moving in the wind, the white of the used car's body, black trim all around, black roof. But most of all I saw the inhabitants of this floating microcosm: two aimless parasites and a self-deluded captain, steering south in search of treasure; the one-eyed "pirate ship," lop-eared and recently scarred, a couple of teeth missing, and the skull and crossbones fender above the flying pavement. I was amused, as is sometimes hard to be on a day like this day, and began to see Mike's side of the "reality" we so often argued about. Man it was funny: here we were in this flapping, unsteady pirate ship, the crew half-asleep and burning through a sea of wet, with no destination and no home. I saw the reality of the thing with great humor, with the captain steering us back and forth in tight arcs across the yellow equator, looking for a thrill that eluded him at every turn. It was really quite funny.

As I drowsed, smiling at my fantasy, the sun finally poked through the clouds. I was immediately awake and more excited, more aware of the dark brown coastline below and of great bright spots on the sea. I left my dream and began to again live my reality, sitting upright in the seat and cranking my neck all around to get the feel of things.

"Hey, Larry, why don't we pull over and try to get down to the beach for a while?"

Larry looked over smugly, his hands tight on the wheel, no humor in his eyes. "Hmmmm..." He wanted to make more miles.

"Yeah, Larry," Mike said, "how about a stop in one of these dink towns and see what's going on around here?"

"Aahhh... I don't know."

There was a short silence as all three of us tried to calculate Larry's mind on this matter.

"Look, Larry," I said, "this driving is too much. Let's get out and smell the ocean for a while."

Larry was resistant. I wanted to stop, but was so pleased to have a ride through all this damp weather.

"I don't know. I've got to make so many miles every day or I won't be able to see all the stuff I want."

So there it was. And it was the final straw for Mike and me. Larry was zooming across the country in his blond automobile, counting the miles and seeing as much highway as he could before returning to the factory, where he could brag about "the Wild West" he had conquered (and maybe the weirdo hitchhikers "out there"). I rolled down the window.

"How far did you want to go today?"

"Well, I'm supposed to make it into California before I stop."

"Hey, that's not too bad. Maybe we can get there before sunset and walk around a little then. It's almost only three now."

"Yeah, I figure just a couple of hours and we'll hit the border."

Shit, so he planned on crossing into California, and I knew from consulting the map that if he didn't like the first town, it would be a long drive to the second one.

My bearded friend from San Francisco came to my rescue. "Look, Larry, another hitchhiker just told me about a great camping spot on the border of Oregon and California. Would you wanna stop there for the night?"

Larry was hesitant. He didn't want to fall into any traps. "Well, if I *like* it, maybe we can."

His words sewed the deal shut. If he didn't like it, he was going the rest of the way by himself.

We finished the afternoon, which was not long, with the sky alternately clearing and clouding, our minds wandering with the road. We all practiced the mental trick of allowing ourselves to be bored. On what level we were busy being bored is another question, but the ride was not unpleasant, and the miles fell beneath us without anxiety. Finally, we neared the border.

I stared nervously for the "signs" our hitchhiker friend had given me. Finally, I saw the proper old, battered road sign and the open, flat area of the beach, and I signaled to Mike that we were there. We asked Larry to pull over.

The beach looked like an abandoned airfield, with a long, flat, hard area making a plateau about halfway between the road and the water. In later conversations, a couple of people on the beach agreed tentatively that this indeed might be a landing strip, but no one ever seemed sure. We pleaded with Larry to pull down a gravel drive, and he complied.

From the road, a couple of vehicles had been visible among the trees and foliage on the sandy coast. However, as Larry grudgingly pulled his car down onto the dirt strip, I gritted my teeth at the sight of deep ruts and rocks in this roadway. But without hesitation, our brave captain continued into the deep foliage, with the road dropping suddenly and bending to the right down to the beach. Finally, we arrived at the calm of the hard-packed sand.

And *Wow*! This looked *nice*! We enjoyed the last of the sun, as a cool cloud cover moved in, and we could see two or three bands of other gypsies along the beach. It was a haven for penniless travelers. Mike and I were immediately at home.

It was a very fine place because of the beach and its abundance of driftwood, but the secret ingredient was that the plateau of the landing strip cut the wind off to a long, narrow area between it and the trees. It was an ideal campsite, and we turned to our driver.

Larry was staring off across the beach, the plateau, and through the trees. He turned slowly to us with a knowing grin and said quietly, "You always get the best spots when you have a car." But he intended to drive on. I was flabbergasted. Mike simply turned to watch the gray waves sloshing in.

With a minimum of conversation, we lifted our bags out of the car and picked up wood as we meandered and headed toward the narrow, nearly windless strip of sand to set up for the night.

Chapter Twenty-Nine

Divorce

As it turned out, Larry did stay in camp with us that blustery night, blissfully consuming our meager rations (I suppose in repayment for the long ride) both at dinner and in the morning. After eating that night, we took crackers and cheese with us up the beach to visit other caravans, which proved a delight.

Here on this pauper's beach were some of the most generous people I've ever met, very welcoming and loving. The camps were quiet, with maybe a transistor radio playing, and we gathered news, shared food and marijuana, and generally relaxed into a tribal calm.

I kept noticing our friend Larry out of the corner of my eye, and with each noticing, my calm was disturbed. He was constantly on the prowl, often at the edge of the firelight, constantly eating. Occasionally, he would ask in a voice just a degree too loud for another beer, and I felt embarrassed to have him as part of our little group.

After visiting several camps, and partaking and sharing, we returned empty-handed to our own campsite and prepared to settle in. Larry was euphoric, commenting again and again on the free beer. He paced back and forth in the firelight (as Mike I lay against an ancient log), practicing what he would say to his fellow workers when he returned to Minnetonka. I felt of a separate race from him.

Finally, the beer took over, and Larry crawled into his backseat to sleep it off. Mike and I were stoned, said little as the fire burned down to embers, then crawled into our tiny abode.

In the morning, I awoke to the sound of Larry rooting though our bags, and Mike and I joined him in eating the last of our food. The day was very young, but Larry had a goal to reach. He repeatedly exhorted us to pack up and get in the car, until he realized we weren't joining him. With brief, awkward "goodbyes," Larry turned his battered ship around and lumbered through the thin morning mist back to the highway. I relaxed deeply, satisfied with food and with the end of my irritation with Larry. We could hear him as he hit the Coast Highway pavement: a brief screech of tires, the engine roaring with hunger, off to consume more of America.

Mike and I stayed at that place for several days. We walked into a little town to get more food, but mainly we were sustained by the kindness of others on the beach. No one else actually left during those happy carefree days, and I wonder, even now, if they are still there in the mist.

Chapter Thirty

End of the Innocence

We fucked up bad in Northern California. One of the other hitchhikers on the same ramp as we, a guy appropriately nicknamed "Dizzy," had some weed with him, and so I walked down to the nearest neon-lit convenience store and coughed up three dollars for beer. When the sun went down, we were already loaded, and he, having just a little more money than we, walked down and got more to drink. We found a spot that we thought was out of sight, and we passed out more than we went to sleep. When I awoke the next morning, sleeping bag over my head, it was to the odd sound of a big car engine idling nearby. Peeping out, I saw a Highway Patrol officer bending over to pick up a plastic baggie. I just slid the sleeping bag back over my head... the baggie held Dizzy's weed and a little brass pipe.

We were hustled down to the little town that served as the county seat, and I experienced being more and more isolated as the day wore on. The booking process was obscene... they don't even let you *pee* by yourself during those things! I was so nervous at times I was shaking. Hung-over, hungry, disheveled and a without doubt ripe to the nose, I was "Exhibit A" for what was wrong with the country. Mike tried to mouth some words to me across the room at one point, but I didn't get it, and the cops put a stop to that in a hurry. They separated all of us, and I literally never saw our man Dizzy again. I'm grateful to this day that they allowed Mike and me to remain together for our ordeal.

After giving us a little inventory sheet of our stuff (one sleeping bag, green; one rucksack, green; one water jug, etc.), we were ushered into the county jail which, I learned later, had been built in the 1800s. It was no doubt very beautiful when viewed from the outside.

First, the inner, heavy, iron-bar door swung closed behind us, and then the outer, heavy, solid-steel door slid shut. (It had a thick five-by-five-foot square of glass for visitors.) We were presented with our new home: sterile, gray, nothing but steel and concrete, and an ancient steam radiator. I felt like I had just stepped off a Tilt-A-Whirl.

The great thing about being booked early in the day was that all the inmates were still asleep... there was only one old, skinny guy sitting at one of the two long, steel "picnic tables" in the center of the room. After a few moments of hesitation, Mike and I shuffled to the first cell on the right. It was empty, and the kindly old guy (name of Bob) spoke a few words to let us know it was okay for us to bunk there. Mike took the bottom and I took the top... there wasn't much to make a home of, a couple of very slim foam mattresses on the steel sleeping platforms, two rough wool blankets, and pillows that might have been used as flotation devices. I have to admit, though, I felt a little better in the cell with just the two of us than in the general cell block, despite the twenty-four-hour glare of the bare bulb outside our bars. There was a walkway for the guards around the perimeter of all the cells, and the outer wall of the cells was made of bars, so they could look in on us at any time. Above the walkway burned bright, bare light the clock around.

Eventually, we went back to the common area, and we were thrilled to find a tiny TV at the very end of the second long picnic table... Mike actually touched it, which elicited a hissed warning from Old Bob: "Best be careful; that belongs to the gent in that cell there!" It had never occurred to either of us that there could be TV in a county jail, much less one privately owned. We retreated to our cell to talk and try to nap... at this point, sleeping was difficult.

We had a pretty good couple of days, making kinda friends with some of the other inmates, including the "Bull-of-the-Woods" (a car thief) and his minion (who had been nabbed at the same time), Old Bob who was former Army, and a handful of other locals. Old Bob tried to teach us how to wash our clothes in a bucket, but he added too much bleach, and when we went to wring out my shorts, "*Riiiiiip!*" those became history. I didn't have much in the way of clothes to start with, so the loss of my underwear was a troubling blow. We also received much informal legal advice from the boys on the block, and sadly for Mike and me, we followed it.

After three days of lima beans and baloney sandwiches (prepared by the Sherriff's wife, who was on a very tight budget to feed the prisoners), Mike and I had our trial and then were marched back into the same cell block: "thirty days in the hole" as the band Humble Pie would later sing. I was at first dumbfounded... I had been smoking pot for a couple of years and had come to assume that it was going to be legal shortly. I just couldn't believe that we had been given thirty long days in this cold and unforgiving cell block. I was later to learn that we were extremely lucky, that the state had just moved possession of marijuana from a felony to a misdemeanor, and if we'd been picked up a few months earlier, we'd have been facing some real time. I sat, dizzy, on my bunk; and time, at that very moment, made its contrarian decision to slow down.

"Doing time" is a phrase that you hear on TV about being in prison, and I soon learned what that phrase means. Being cut off from fresh air, green grass, and sunshine is one thing, but the *real* challenge is passing the time. The cops allowed Mike and me to keep the one book each of us was traveling with when we came in. It was a shock how quickly these were consumed... and re-consumed. I had happened upon a shocking newish book from England, *A Clockwork Orange*, which Mike and I read over and over again, gaining more understanding with each read, and then quizzed each other over the Newspeak words and phrases. There were also a few tattered paperbacks on the steel benches, which we read much too quickly. Of course, there are playing cards in county stir, and of course, we played ad nauseam. The big guy at the end with the TV would turn it on in the evenings, sometimes (believe me, nobody was to touch his TV but him...), but as Mike and I were by the farthest cell from TV guy, what we mainly got was a grainy, gray blur from our end of the tables. Man, there wasn't even a radio in that place. There was a tall clock tower over the county courthouse, and I could see the clock face (through one set of bars, across the guard's walkway, and out through a window and another set of bars) from my bunk. Many times, I found myself staring at the big clock and just counting the seconds until I got to sixty, grateful that another minute of my thirty days had passed. Not a good memory.

The most depressing part for me was the jailhouse tattoos. The boys chided us for not joining them, but I had learned a strong prejudice against tattoos from my mother when I was young, so I held back, in part to get a feel for the quality of the work. "The Bull" and his apprentice took apart a couple of disposable ink pens and forced the ink out of the tubes into a bottle cap. They then unbent a safety pin, which they dipped in the ink, and then

124

used this primitive system to mark themselves. You can imagine how slow this process was, and I got bored after a while and wandered back to my bunk. When I once again stopped by to see progress on the skin art, I was horrified to see a Christian cross, crooked and uneven, on the apprentice's fish-belly forearm... he was busy filling in the middle of the cross solid, and later in the day would outline it with a dashed line... the whole mess reeked of dim-wittedness, and I gave thanks for my Mother's admonitions. To this day, I can spot a jailhouse tat a mile away... just awful.

Sleep is the main antidote to doing time in a place like this, so sleep we did, whether we needed it or not. I can remember looking up at my big clock face and wondering if it was six in the morning or six at night... all we tried to do was be unconscious to the passing of time. Small events marked the endless march of minutes: someone going to trial; someone being booked in. Mainly it was tedium. One nice thing was that the bunk "mattresses" fit very precisely into the cell door openings, giving us a little privacy and quiet. We also learned a way to get an extra blanket after a guy left, and then we'd use rolls of toilet paper jammed between it and a set of bars to cover our bar-wall, to keep out the light and let us sleep more. In an act that caused me to hate cops for several years, a big jailer punched down our door, pulled our blanket off the wall, and stormed out with "our" stuff, muttering threats... it was June, and when a rainy front moved in, I could've really used that second blanket.

Folks were pretty friendly most of the time, and we even felt pity for some of the drunk drivers that passed through: bewildered, hung-over, nicely dressed, and vaguely desperate. Mike and I found ourselves caught up in the game of giving legal advice to people who found themselves in this bizarre world. It was a form of entertainment, delivered with trial-lawyer certainty. I learned that this was only a form of entertainment, and I had fallen for it.

The only scrape we got in was when the Bull-of-the-Woods and his crony burst into our cell one night. The two of them punched down our mattress "door" and strode in belligerently. The Bull held a floppy Bible in one hand and the crony a long steel nail. I don't know where the nail came from, and I had never before in my life considered a nail as a weapon, but in this stark landscape, things took on a new, sinister shape. I had the sense that the two of them were loaded, but my mind couldn't reconcile that with being in the pokey... I couldn't imagine how they could have gotten or used anything to get high. Anyhow, Bull-the-Bible-Thumper was ranting in a strange way, looking out the bars of the outside cell wall, when he suddenly turned to us on our bunks and began to describe in horrid detail how he was going to sexually abuse us. My stomach gripped as if I had the shits, and my mouth went dry. The minion was muttering strangely and kept thrusting the nail forward, not really violent-like but kinda slow, and this, somehow, was even worse. The Bull kept it up for several minutes, and this turned out to be a good thing... both Mike and I regained our wits. Our salvation and defense arrived from the muse of humor... Mike was able to sneak a little comment in, which caused a little pause... and I was able to build on that with another... a thin cloud of doubt crossed The Bull's face, his eyebrows pinching a bit. Mike made another, more substantial joke. Minion paused, a little unsure, and then (thank God!) The Bull added his own joke. We carried on for a few minutes, the whole chilling thing becoming food for banter, and then they were gone. I lay back down, recounting in my mind where the nearest guard was stationed, realizing that we were on our own back there, and giving thanks for Mikey's sense of humor.

Soon after that chilling event, the jailers admitted a second "bull," and we could smell a real problem, right from the get-go. This guy was hugely muscled and hadn't been missing any meals. Our local bull was pasty and soft from months and months of sitting in County... but his mind still saw himself as a bruiser. The trouble started small enough... the new bull asserting his rights, the old bull making a little comment to his side-kick, obviously pointed at the new bull. I was in my cell when things went bad and had a cold lesson in how lonely we were back in that cell block... the guards really didn't give a shit what happened. Things got ugly, and things got protracted... after the defeat of the old bull, the punishment went on for a while. It was loud and bloody and frightening, and I barely went out of the cell for two days after.

In a real surprise, Mike and I were called out after twenty-one days to meet someone from the District Attorney's office. We were taken outside the barred door, then outside the solid door, then marched upstairs to a nice little meeting room with cushions on the chairs. Sunlight poured in, and I felt a tad bedazzled. The nice thirty-something man with a tie asked us questions about our time in jail: were we in danger of being repeat offenders? and on like that for ten or fifteen minutes.

He then offered us our release.

I was so stupefied that I asked the man to let us talk about it for a minute, and he obligingly left the room.

"What's there to talk about?" said Mike in a slightly panicked voice, his eyes wide. He wanted out bad, but I was afraid there was some hidden catch to this miracle... what would we have to pay in order to obtain our freedom? Mike saw none, and so we agreed with Tie Man, and in an unbelievable swirl, we were soon given back our possessions (checked against our little inventory sheets) and unceremoniously stepped out of the behemoth. We had barely said a word to our block-mates. It was a startling June day. My mind reeled. From outside, the sandstone prison *was* beautiful, surrounded by neon grass. We started walking toward the highway.

We spent the night in a little hollow in a dark town park, about three-quarters of the way from the jail to the highway. We couldn't stop talking about our good luck, and the sense of freedom and fresh air kept us giddy until we slept.

Chapter Thirty-One

The Golden Road

The Coast Highway in Northern California is a near-carnival ride of constant sweeping in-and-out as the road hugs the shore. Sometimes Highway 1, and sometimes 101, the Coast Highway has near-mythical status among hitchhikers, as there is a world of the unusual and unexpected always just around the next bend: great driftwood sculptures, surprising rock formations, arts communities, people striving to live counter-culturally... it's a very lively ride.

As Mike and I wound our way near to San Francisco, we both noticed a particular peninsula of high land jutting out into the ocean. As our eyes swept back-and-forth, we gradually resolved that this should be our home for the night, as it was late afternoon... and the finger of high rock just called to us.

Our driver was a bit stunned by our request and a little nervous, as there wasn't much room to pull off the road, but Mike and I piled out in a hurry and let our driver get back to it.

We were enveloped by a nearly silent calm.

We had chosen well, if almost entirely by chance: the peninsula, high above the ocean, was heavy with vegetation. There was a trace of a path out to the point, and along the path a beautiful little bowl beneath overhanging trees in which to camp... it really was a dream come true. We were able to set up the tent and get our bags laid out, then enjoy the sunset, the view impeded only by a beautiful flight of pelicans.

The real excitement began after we settled into camp. Enfolded in our natural womb, with the earth around and the trees over, with the washing waves overwhelming any traffic noise, and with a little pot of steaming noodles over the coals, the great lights of the city gradually emerged to the southeast. At first not really noticeable, perhaps due to a long tongue of fog which protruded from the wide mouth of the Golden Gate, the lights began to gradually glow altogether, to create an orb of golden light in our future.

I was mesmerized.

We of course had no weed or alcohol with us, but the setting and the scene within the mouth of the bay created a wondrous natural high. We sat comfortably supported and just gazed into the golden lights beyond. I felt sure that we were on the verge of finding what we'd come so far to discover. The city appeared as a surreal treasure, ready for us to reach out and grasp it, possibly the end of our cold and hungry trail.

To this day, that remains the favorite campsite of my life: we were fed, safe, and surrounded by nature's wonder: within our grasp, a beautiful dream, or if not a dream, at least the truth that we had been searching for. I always remember that night as a warm glow, like campfire coals.

Chapter Thirty-Two
The Promised Land, Part One

In San Francisco, Mike and I found the end of the American road for us. We found that we had matured to the point of independence, and life began to change. On a beautiful, warm, foggy, and damp day, we rolled into town in the back of our favorite type of vehicle: a pickup truck. We surveyed the great Golden Gate above and around us as we rode slowly through the heavy traffic crossing the bridge.

"I thought we were going to *walk* across!" I shouted above the din of hundreds of buzzing tires.

"So did I!" Mike smiled back. He was happy and dirty and his golden, curly hair pressed before his eyes in the wind.

"I wish to hell we'd get our shit *organized*!" I was barely audible in the din of the bridge-crossing.

"Ah, Eddie..." Mike was laughing at me again, and I was a little hurt at our not walking across the orange bridge.

Orange? Shit! After all this waiting and thinking, only to cross into the land of enchantment on an orange bridge! Mike considered this funny, too.

"I heard they start at one end, paint to the other side, and then start all over again," Mike said. Considering the damp fog closing in, I wasn't surprised at that.

However, we were both suddenly surprised at the slowing of the truck, and we peered around our respective sides of the cab to see what the matter was. A toll booth. After a short stop and a lurch forward, we suddenly curved around a bus stop on our right and stopped in a small parking lot. Here, our assumptions made us fools.

"Where you guys headed?"

We had consulted a map earlier and had decided to take the main road, the one which crossed the bridge, all the way into town. We assumed that the driver and her friends were going down a side road into Golden Gate Park.

"Well, this'll be good enough," Mike shouted, and we quickly got busy with unloading the packs and all our things that had shook loose in the bed of the pickup.

"Thanks a lot!" we were still hollering when the driver looked at us narrowly, hesitated a moment, then put it in gear.

"So long," she yelled and opening her up, turned the truck a quick one-eighty and sped down the highway toward our destination.

I suddenly felt deflated. I wanted to go where she was going, and now stupidly, I stood where no one could pick us up, when we might've continued our ride into the Promised Land. It was ridiculous.

Gradually, we recognized a single point where the cars hesitated... passing through the toll booths, they had just a moment to look us over, and finally Mikey reeled in a driver with big-city indifference who rolled us way into town. Without really caring one way or the other, he took a slight detour to drop us off in the Haight district, which we didn't know from Stinson Beach.

The driver had nailed us: the Haight was what we needed to be dropped into, although we really had to swim just to keep our heads above the roiling waters of that wild scene... half-ghetto, half-bohemian, the area was a tapestry which changed with every angle of sunlight and every flickering streetlight: a kaleidoscope of colors, lights, new people, new thoughts and feelings. We stayed at free crash pads, then found work, then found lovers... I was split wide open and drank and drank and drank from the unceasing flow of the new, the wild, the gorgeous, and the vain.

Although we lived together, Mike and I began to argue more often; we started spending time with different crowds and started drifting apart. I was drinking almost nightly, despite my lack of money, and just getting by at work... and I didn't care.

I fell in with a "Grateful Dead" crowd, which appealed to my dreams of mind expansion through drugs, but although Mike would join me now and then, he never fell into the tie-dye scene the way I did, and I always felt that he looked down on "my" group a little. I found a new life, and between braying at the stars and listening to music, I mainly chased moon-faced girls.

Although I had a few lovers in San Francisco, these were of the one-night-stand variety, mostly drunken blurs, and I don't remember their names. Mike, on the other hand, had fallen hard for one particular woman, and they (despite the bohemian prohibition against pairing up) gradually became a couple. They became more serious in most every way, and I just stopped seeing them around. I didn't really mind.

I found myself more and more adrift in the Haight. I gradually realized that at parties I practiced "hit and run" with most everyone I met: I'd stop for a few minutes of conversation and then drift away at the first opportunity. I felt more alone in the midst of a crowd than anywhere else. I didn't know what to do with myself... I found less and less joy in the wild parties, less and less naïve-awe of the poets and artists who populated our 'hood, and more and more lonesomeness, feeling a stranger even in the throngs of wild children whom I looked much like.

Finally, Mike moved in with his woman, leaving me alone in our bare "cell," and I knew with great, bare-bulb, shocking clarity that my time in San Francisco was closing. I had nothing to show for my time here, nothing but memories... my adrenaline was drained away, the lights no longer shown for me, and without really meaning to, I simply walked out.

Chapter Thirty-Three
Wandering Jew

Hitchhikers sometimes leave messages for each other, penciled on the back of street signs where one would most logically stand. After walking to the nearest freeway ramp, I found myself in an impossible situation… the traffic roared past on the curving ramp, without a single wide spot for one to pull over. After thirty panicked minutes, I finally checked the back of several signs and found the following: "Don't stand here, stupid, cross over to the other side." I had to look around and allow the meaning to soak in… across the street was a steep hill, and cars stopped at the intersection would be backed waaaay up the hill before the green light came on, when a mad rush of cars cascaded onto the freeway ramp. However, if I crossed the road, I would have a chance with the first several cars that were waiting for the light… the number of potential rides was much less, but the possibility of physically getting into a stopped vehicle was much better.

I waited a long time.

In what remains to this day a shock to me, a taxi driver waved me over to his piss-yellow ride, with his thumb indicating that I should climb in back… I didn't question, I was just so glad to get a ride. He was heading to the airport, and although he said he had a fare waiting for him there, the constant ticking of his meter caused my stomach to twist in two by the time we got to that exit… I kept thinking he expected something from me, but then I didn't, and I had nothing to give him anyway. So I jumped out and began one of the strangest parts of the trip.

At first even *I* didn't realize what I was doing, but gradually it became clear that I had nowhere to go and no schedule for getting there. I felt divorced from all I knew and from all things I had known… I simply went where the drivers were going, surprising them over and over by saying that I would just go where they were headed. Some of the drivers were a bit suspicious, but I really didn't want anything from them aside from the transport, so they would gradually relax and chat a while before dropping me off. Two-lanes, four-lanes, or more-lanes, it really no longer mattered to me. I had initially thought that I would go to Los Angeles and enjoy the warmth there… there were images in my head of beach girls, surfers, and the mystery of Big Sur on the way south, but I was just drifting. I happened to drift a bit east as I headed generally south. I slept in forests and in farmers' fields. If I was hungry, or the night looked bad, I developed a little patter for the driver: Did they know of a good place to sleep near to where they were dropping me? Any place for cheap food? And sometimes they'd take me in… I slept under dining tables, on couches, on living room floors. Sometimes the wives would be a little shaky until I chatted with them a while… they always came around.

I worked the odd day of labor, sometimes got a shower, really didn't give a shit what was going on around me, and drank way too much beer.

The only noticeable event was nearly getting shot by a guy I thought was the blandest character I'd met on my journey. I had just gotten a short one-or-two-exit ride from three "Deadheads" in a VW microbus, a rolling caricature of California, when almost immediately Driver Bland picked me up. The hippies were headed east to a dead-end in a national park, so I just kept heading south toward Bakersfield. The new driver immediately began to ask me a lot of questions, which was unusual. I asked him a few, too, including about his radio mounted below the dash, which was silent. We relaxed into a ride of maybe twenty miles, then he pulled off to let me out at an intersection. As I reached between my knees for my bag, though, things changed fast:

"Put your hands on the dashboard!"

I couldn't believe my ears, so I must've looked shocked when I turned my head to look at the guy. He had a pistol trained on my head.

"Hands... on the dashboard!"

Bland Boy identified himself as a narcotics detective and asked a series of staccato questions to which I had no answers. I thought for sure it had to do with the hippies, so I immediately began to plead my case: "Look man, I don't even *know* those guys, they just gave me a *ride*, see..."

Bland Driver cut me off, his face growing more and more agitated as he peppered me with questions... I actually rehearsed in my mind what being shot was going to feel like. Finally (I'm still surprised by this!) I asked the man for an ID, and sure enough he produced an official-looking badge. I was dumbfounded, thought perhaps it had to do with my troubles up north, tried to calm the cop down, and tried to get my bearings.

I must've said or done something to let him know I was harmless, as he slowly changed colors from purple to red, finally asking me for my bag, which I quickly handed to him. With my hands visible on the dashboard, he came around the front of the car and had me step out to be searched. I actually had a driver's license on me, which he soon checked, and the situation began to resemble something closer to "normal" again.

I ended up at a police station, but by that time Detective Bland had settled himself down. There was actually an FBI agent on the case in question, and it took him less than a minute to check me out and confirm that no, I wasn't the guy they were looking for. I was put back in the unmarked car, and Bland drove me back out to the highway, explaining all the while that he had been on the scene of a horrific drug-deal-gone-bad in which two young children were killed, and that I fit the description of the perpetrator. Part of my problem was that with my T-shirt sleeves rolled up, a nasty scar was revealed, which was much like that of the man they hunted.

Without a word of apology from Bland, I was dumped back on the highway, with my head spinning to the point where I had to just sit down off the road for a while.

I've had a number of people pull guns on me during my travels, but that was the one time I was sure I was gonna get shot, and by the cops, of all people!

Chapter Thirty-Four

Alone on the Way

There's a particular kind of loneliness that envelops the solo traveler, whether standing by the side of a howling freeway ramp, lying alone at night in an unknown woods, or in the mix with a horde of strangers, say, at a filthy bus terminal. Alone, you might be engaged in conversation with a driver, a car load of riders, or even just getting directions when lost... but the conversation never sinks in below the skin level... it's only on the surface, never anything meaningful, sadly, much like home.

Traveling solo can have a specter-like effect... one has the ability to pass through places, it seems like right through solid walls, without anyone else noticing. If I don't stand out in front of you with my thumb extended, looking you dead in the eye, you'll probably blow right past me. Likewise, a raggedy waif in a crowded place doesn't attract interest from others... rather, people quickly look away, and the waif passes through without any scrutiny at all. Feels like an advantage for quite some time, but gradually this invisibility becomes a burden: a chafing, mild, unrelenting pain.

The other thing is that alone, you have nobody to watch your stuff, or your back. So if you need to use the can in the afore-mentioned filthy bus station, you have to haul your stuff with you. There you are sitting on the john, with all your worldly possessions crammed in there with you, and you can't relax because you're afraid that a hand is gonna reach up over the door (if you hung anything on the hook) or from under the divider, and you might have to bolt after them to get your shit back… so it's a challenge just getting the body to evacuate in that situation… so that's another thing about traveling alone.

At first, this loneliness felt like a thrill, an absolute thrill: to be out on my own, no one to answer to, no one to accommodate, no fuss and no pain. But gradually that thrill of absolute freedom began to dissolve into a vague ennui. Taken in large enough doses, it acquired a gray-colored sadness. Not like it pushed me to want camaraderie more, and not that I suddenly felt like settling down and getting a job and a woman, but only the full, flinching admission of the actual state of being human: alone and fundamentally unable to communicate meaningfully with others.

What did emerge over time is that I wanted to participate in the charade of human interaction, to try, to at least pretend that we can communicate… *that* became more important than actual meaningful dialogue.

The road can strip you down like that: clothing, hygiene, sense of who you are, sense of belonging, all of it… it all comes into question and can only be answered by the traveler himself: What is real? What is the illusion? Do I really care? Ultimately, for me, the response came involuntarily, rose up from within: eventually, I just didn't care about the universal truth of human existence… I just wanted to participate in the dance, charade or no charade.

My journey began to bend of its own will after that, gradually turning, slowly, slowly back toward where I'd come from, back home to where I at least knew the names of the people I pretended with.

Chapter Thirty-Five

The Games We Played

Much of the time on the road is unremarkable. In the city, it's a constant rumble of cars speeding by without a look; in the country, it's the silence interrupted by the occasional vehicle. It can get boring and tedious, depending on the weather, as the weather, good and bad, can make for very interesting times.

But when all else fails, you have to come up with your own games to play.

The usual "car" games are a decent pastime, especially if you are traveling with a partner and can have a little competition: "I'm thinking of..." is a good one as are variations on "twenty questions." But "I spy with my little eye" can get as tedious as boredom itself, especially in a sparse landscape, and is best left to young kids.

Reading while at a lonely crossroads is possible, as long as you don't get too caught up in it and forget to make eye contact with the drivers going by. Certain activities are much more "western," simply because you can find yourself stranded for a good long while out there... you gotta be prepared to bunk down where you are!

Now every hitchhiker worth his salt knows about "the can game," which is simply a discarded tin can into which pebbles are tossed from afar, again, much more entertaining with a sidekick... but it can be stimulating on one's own. I got pretty good at it, with the real contest making a distance shot.

Also, back then, a hitchhiker could count on getting high somewhere along the line, not every day, mind you, but often enough to break the boredom. So the most interesting game that comes to my mind was in the California desert, when I got stoned to the bone with my temporary pal Tim, and we played "hide and seek" in a spot where there was a utility pole, a big electric box on the ground, and really nothing else to hide behind. We went on playing for a couple of hours, screaming, with the tears rolling down our faces... and as you can guess, we slept in a nearby dry creek bed that night and woke up hungry and confused.

But the games and my nonchalance gradually wore away to expose the aching nerve of my confusion. I didn't know where I was going, which should have meant complete freedom, but instead I found myself unable to sleep, worrying myself about I-knew-not-what, and at all times carrying a certain weight which I could not name. The beer was supposed to sooth all this, but I found myself increasingly maudlin, beer or no beer, as I wandered my way south, then east.

I wanted direction to my Promised Land, but I simply had no direction. I wanted the wandering to have meaning, but it had no meaning.

Part Two

Chapter Thirty-Six

The Middle, Part One

The middle of the journey feels like a blur to me now.

I got to Las Vegas in an unexpected way... that is, I wasn't intending to go there. As people do, it just happened that I got a long ride, got curious about the city from talking with the driver, and thought I'd better see this freak show for myself. I still remember the lights, as at first we saw them in the distance as a glow, then the constellations of them in the middle distance, and finally the dizzying pulsations when rolling down the main drag. My driver and I had been together a long time, and he had come to trust me (and I him) so I left my things in his car in the back parking lot and entered a jangling casino from there. I was dazed with it immediately and never really took to the distraction of it all. My driver went off to "real" gambling, while I lurked around the cheap slots, gratefully milking a drink or two from the cutest waitress, as I tried to keep my dollar or two going for an hour.

I had formed an impression of Vegas from TV, and I expected to see fancy cars, with secret agent men in tuxedoes, and models in gowns. What I got was Ma and Pa Kettle from Wisconsin: overweight, poorly-dressed, bleary-eyed, black-socks-and-sandals, and the whitest fish-belly skin on God's earth. In surveying the crowd, I feared that half of them would drop from a heart attack or other age-related illness before they could get on the flight back home. I stared in slack-jawed wonder as another of my illusions shattered to the ground. It was a stunning evening.

My driver returned in a great, boozy haze, having won a little money and having drunk both free and "bought" liquor. He was so magnanimous and wobbly that he threw an arm around me and, as we stumbled out to the car, invited me to his friend's house for the night. Although the desert air felt balmy even at midnight, the offer of a roof was too sweet to pass up. Soon we had roused his lady friend, and she, with some misgivings, let us in. He took me on a brief, inebriated tour of the little condo, which included the most outrageous bright-red, heart-shaped bed imaginable, and then I quickly, gratefully settled in on the couch. Drowsiness overtook me as I half-listened to the rhythmic creaking upstairs.

In the morning, Lady Friend awoke quite early. Although I could tell she was just a hair defensive, her curiosity got the better of her, and she made the two of us coffee and breakfast while my driver slept it off upstairs. She picked and picked at me, more and more curious about what I was doing and why. I could tell by the glint in her eye that she found me interesting, and as I hadn't basked in *that* glow in some time, I deeply enjoyed it. Her quizzing finally satisfied, she shared just a bit of her life, and sure enough, I became interested in life behind the curtain in this strangest of American cities. Lady Friend hurried upstairs to get dressed, as she worked an early shift, but she made it clear that I should stay on another day if I liked, and that she could certainly find a clean white boy some work if I wanted to clean up.

My driver was an Olympic-quality sleeper and as the day wore on, I began to entertain the thought of myself in a colorful vest and bow tie, shuffling and dealing cards and carrying on banter with the wealthy gamblers. By noon, I had decided to stay on and learn the trade, and if they didn't need Blackjack dealers,

145

then I'd gladly be a bartender... I figured the tips alone would keep me afloat for a long time.

The other thing that happened is that Lady Friend (who, it turned out, was named Janet) took me and my driver (Charlie) to a house party where I met a whole lot of folks who worked in the casinos. These were some hard-drinking and frankly very beautiful people, and it wasn't long before I had my heart set on one or two of the girls in Janet's circle.

You can imagine the rest of this story: unable to find a glamour job, I was soon working in food service, dumping huge buckets of chow into troughs for the feeding tourists. Although I was all smiles and courtesy on the outside, within a day I had joined my co-workers in an intense hatred for the people who paid our wages, considering them untutored hicks, despite the fact that I had just arrived there myself. I quickly fell in love with, and moved in with, a beautiful girl named Marie, who had the most beautiful young children. I must say that although I believe I did love Marie, I fell more deeply in love with the kids than her. The girls were tentative with me at first; I think they'd been through one too many boyfriends that they liked better than Mom did, but gradually they came to accept and then (I might say) love me.

Finally, a slice of heaven.

And you can probably tell the rest of this story as well: the days got to be so repetitive that they just flowed together. I became devoted to the kids to the point that I was working my ass off, even securing two raises, all in an effort to provide for their welfare. For her part, Marie, despite the two kids, could still wear an Asian-inspired cocktail dress, with a side slit all the way up to her waist, and bring home fabulous cash tips from the casino where she worked.

So there you have it: living in an exciting town with a beautiful woman, getting a regular paycheck, and being proud of feeding the kids. I could have gone on like that forever, really, with Marie and I just playing the roles assigned. The days and the drudgery blurred into weeks, and then the weeks into years. We were moderately happy, enjoying small outings and events as a family, with memorable times sprinkled in. The girls were as bright as the smooth stones in the bottom of a creek, life flowing over them at high speed, so school was no problem and, like I said, we were moderately happy.

I couldn't really say how long I, and we, spent in this dream world: the lights flashing, the days flowing past, the girls growing. But at some point, things began to sour between Marie and me. Maybe it was my drinking which, although modest by tourist standards, had become a daily affair. From my side, I felt that Marie just came to take me for granted, like I would always be there. She gradually stopped noticing what I did for the kids and how much I contributed to the household, and our sex life dropped off. The glitter just started to go out of the whole city for me.

I had found a small watering hole that was more or less reserved for locals. It was dark and cool, amber lights against the walls, with a tight-lipped barman. I found myself hanging around in there a lot more than I should have: sometimes after work for hours, not giving a shit whether or not I was expected home for dinner. Sometimes *before* work if I worked the late shift, but I had to watch that, as the manager at the hotel kept a close eye on us all. I have to admit, I went home with a couple of the girls after the bar closed... not that I'm proud of it or that it was even a lot of fun, but it's just what a drunk does when he's feeling pitiful and in need of love. Marie never knew for sure, but right afterwards I was so busy watching her, watching what I said, making sure I didn't smell of the girls and all, that I'm sure she suspected. Things just became a lot more unsteady. To mellow out, I tried smoking pot, including a couple of times before work, but between the insane giggling and the utter fatigue by the end of the shift, I had to cut that out. I liked the pot, but it had gotten so strong by then that I was jumpy and anxious when I smoked it, so it wasn't really doing what I asked of it. So it was easy for me to cut that out.

It's hard to say just when things started really turning sour for me, but between that burrow of a bar, the coldness from Marie, and the suspicion at work, I gradually found myself up against it. My mantra became "Just Leave Me Alone!" and whether I said it out loud or only to myself, over and over again, the world around me got the message. I began a slow and horrid slide down the black mine shaft of self-pity and despair. I just couldn't see my way out. So much to her relief, Marie finally showed me the way out. Thankfully, the girls weren't home at the time, so we said our goodbyes over the phone a few days later... they were so confused that they didn't know whether to bawl, be strong, or laugh.

That was a tough conversation.

Chapter Thirty-Seven
The Middle, Part Two

I hung around town for a few weeks after Marie put me out, all proud of my independence, carefully informing everyone what a bitch Marie was, letting every girl I met know how single and available I was (which seemed to have the opposite effect than what I intended). But I could feel in my gut that it just wasn't good anymore. I despised the tourists, I despised my low-rent job, I despised my fellow low-rung workers, and finally, I came to despise myself.

In some spiritual programs, they use the term "in denial" for a person who's really sick but won't admit they have a real problem. "Denial" isn't the right word, though. "Unaware" might be a better word, or "numb" or something like that... "Denial" is just too active a word. I was just plain too stupid to know how deep the shit was that I was splashing around in.

I decided that Nevada in general, and Las Vegas in particular, was too fucked up, too dumb, too dead-end for me, and so I started out on the road again, once more with almost nothing: a sleeping bag, a red vinyl gym bag, and a gallon of water. I thought myself very clever for bringing a roll of masking tape with me, and I would use (and reuse) the masking tape to write the name of my next destination on the outside of the bag, so that drivers had an idea of where I was headed. I had a little money in my shoe, but it ate at me that I had spent years, *years*! in Las Vegas, and there I was leaving with probably less than I came into it with; I didn't even have the tent I had borrowed and cared for on my trip out West. This thought chapped my ass for weeks.

I had a couple of friends in Flagstaff, and two more guys in Phoenix that I knew from high school who were rooming together, and all had found work in Arizona. I dunno, I just didn't have any place else to go, and besides, who doesn't love the names "Flagstaff" and "Phoenix"?

Part Three

Chapter Thirty-Eight
Coyote and a Foolish Man

In my distracted state of mind, I inadvertently took a main road headed northeast out of Las Vegas, rather than southeast. I was oblivious to the fact for a shockingly long time. I had no idea of what season it was, as it all seems the same in the desert, but I soon learned that it was spring as I crossed into higher country. The false sparkle of the city fell behind, and I discovered very lonesome country not far from the bustle of Vegas.

I had traveled all the way to St. George, Utah, before I realized my mistake. Thankfully, a driver headed north out of the town, who asked where I was headed, laughed and pointed out that I was headed in the wrong direction. He gave me some specific directions, and I gradually worked my way over to Route 89 and headed south, at last headed toward my destination.

A young Navajo man picked me up in a late-model Ford Mustang, and we chatted in very "white" terms as he sped along the two-lane. He seemed to be a man with his fee in two different universes: one white and one red. Despite his worldliness, he dropped me at a surprisingly primitive crossroads and headed home down a red double-track into the desert. The view was stunning. A deep, red canyon to the west was one of the most spectacular sights of my life. I was later to learn that this was very close to the northern end of the mighty Grand Canyon, a trifle compared to the real thing.

I felt mighty lonesome out there, with the wind a steady companion. There was not much to see, and as I awaited the sounds of approaching cars, I spent a great deal of time just sitting on the blacktop, thinking.

After standing up for a passing car, I noticed (once the car had left me in the dust) a "dog," the color of which matched the desert very closely. He was half-hidden by a low bush, but it was clear that he was eyeing me over. I was at first confused, as I stared into his gold-brown eyes, but then became a bit alarmed as he moved, sometimes quickly, sometimes slowly, in a gradual arc around where I stood waiting.

A game of cat-and-mouse ensued, where I would gradually relax, thinking the coyote (not a dog) had finally left, and then I would notice movement out of the corner of my eye, and there he'd be again, not threatening, not bashful, but just watching, impassive. I was alert for any companion-coyotes joining my cool observer, but none others did. Although I remained alert, I gradually felt that the coyote and I arrived at some type of understanding... I saw myself in him... and I wonder if he saw me in himself.

To my surprise, a station wagon full of Navajo fellas rumbled out of the same desert double-track that the young Navajo man had disappeared into. With a brown-red cloud foaming behind them, they paused at the asphalt road. At first I thought they were hesitant to pull from the beaten double-track onto the high-speed blacktop, but then I realized they were waiting for me.

I was able to hold my gym bag, with my sleeping bag and water jug hanging around me by a length of clothesline, on my lap; my boots rested on a coiled lariat. All of the Navajo wore long sleeves, long pants, and hats and boots.

Probably because I was secretly thrilled to meet honest-to-God Indians, I jabbered away for a full minute, asking their names and sharing mine, where I was from, all that, and on and on...

until I realized that I wasn't eliciting as much as a grunt from anyone else in the car.

We rolled like that, dusty, dark, silent, and hot, without a word, until we reached a little two-lane intersection where we parted ways. I again jabbered my thanks and good wishes, only to be met by a silent wave and another cloud of dust.

I thought later that maybe in that lonely country, a good fella stops to pick you up, if he has room, whether he knows you or not, just because it's the right thing to do. I've seen plenty of folks in the years since, just walking beside the road, and I always think (if I don't have room) that maybe they don't actually need to hitch a ride, that others in this empty country will always stop, just in case their fortunes are reversed someday... I think like that.

Chapter Thirty-Nine

Acey-Duecey

I was at a lonely crossroads in Arizona, feeling pretty lean and grateful for the water I had with me: a rinsed-out plastic gallon milk jug that someone had given me, filled at a gas station a while back. As the jug dropped below half-full, I began to get just a hair nervous about the desert heat, which I was experiencing really for the first time.

Finally, an unusual white man by the name of Ace Brooks, a hell of a guy, really, despite a horrific drinking problem, plucked me from the desert. He was my next ride, after the carload of Navajos, and introduced himself as "Ace," but his real name was "Acel." (I gotta tell you, I don't know how to spell that, but it's pronounced "ace-ul.") His good friends called him "Deuce," just because. He was a wiry, very brown white man, his face deeply wrinkled from the sun, but with bright and lively blue eyes. He was sipping on a beer when he picked me up and smelled like garlic and stale whiskey, so it was no surprise to me when he shared stories of his loves and losses, all of which revolved around drinking. We rolled through the desert for a couple of hours, the windows open and the hot air blasting around us, him occasionally leaning back whilst driving full-tilt to fish the occasional beer out of an ice chest in the backseat. I sipped on mine nice and slow, knowing that sooner or later I was gonna be back out in that frying pan of a desert and not wanting to be sick or parched; but Ace kept up a steady pace, keeping himself cool as we sped along. It was a very pleasing couple of hours, full of conversation, laughs, and comfortable silences.

155

Now, Ace's car wasn't exactly new, the age of it being another manifestation of his bad luck with liquor, women, and ultimately money. The maintenance on said aging vehicle was also neglected, due in large part to my man's preoccupation with those other three things. First he, and then gradually we, began to feel an uncomfortable wobble in the passenger rear quarter of the car, and it became clear that we'd soon have to pull over.

I was feeling just a bit sick, what with the heat, the beer, and the car trouble, and I started to have visions of us just sitting on the side of the sun-blasted blacktop, with not much company passing by. However, in what appeared to me at first as a mirage soon materialized into an honest-to-God trading post/gas station/grocery store on the side of the road. I shook my head in amazement. As we pulled off the road, I noticed a couple of Indian fellas sitting in the sparse shade of the cottonwoods right there, sipping out of paper bags, and giving a hint as to the back-door cash flow for the little enterprise.

I had a sense of us being saved... I really did. Maybe it was the beer. Ace and the man from the garage stood at his rear tire, talking it over and finally deciding on a price to rotate Ace's spare for the failing tire now on the car. I joined Ace at the rear of the car, looking to be of help, and my heart dropped to my stomach when he opened the trunk: there, glittering in the sun like Sinbad's jewels, were dozens, maybe *hundreds*, of broken bottles... the trunk was literally filled to the top with a load of smashed glass! I have wondered a thousand times since that moment why a man would drive such a load of broken glass around all the time, and I have never yet come up with an answer, well, maybe a partial one: I think that glass was like the man's life, and in a peculiar alcoholic way he had as much

156

trouble getting rid of the physical as he did the emotional. It would take an hour to dig all that nasty glass outta there and fish out a questionable spare, and not a work glove between us.

We stood there for a few moments, surveying the situation without speaking. I got a funny feeling that Acel was talking kinda thirsty-like, and on an impulse, I made up my mind.

I began telling Ace how much I enjoyed his company, that I really appreciated the ride, that if he saw me up the road, I hoped he'd pick me up again, that I wished I could help, but I had no real automotive skills, and on like that. But all the time I was moving to the side of the car and fishing out my meager gear. Looping the old clothesline over my shoulder, I turned and gave Ace a handshake and wished him well... he was surprisingly good-natured about it all, and I strode maybe fifteen yards up the road to a little patch of shade to try for another ride.

Over the next day and a half, I really thought I'd see Acel's battered car rumbling toward me, but I never did see him again. It left such a soft spot in my heart, having met and then lost the man. I can only hope that he found his way, jewels or no.

Chapter Forty

The Loneliest Night I Ever Spent

I caught a ride with a great young couple headed south in a VW microbus. They really had the joy of life. We picked up another vagabond along the road, and the four of us rolled along listening to rock-and-roll and shouting above the din of the highway wind. The young couple shared apples with the other pilgrim and me, and we ate them right down to the cores then ate the cores, leaving only the little stems to pitch out the sliding windows. Darkness closed in, but I gave no attention to it. In my delight, I was also oblivious to the changing altitude. Without my realizing it, our little van moved from desert into pine forest and ever-higher altitudes. I was soon to learn what it meant to be on the high Colorado Plateau in early June.

The other hitchhiker was more purposeful than myself and heaved himself and his duffel out at a two-lane, hopeful of getting to his sweetie the next day. I, more uncertain of my exact direction, stayed with the microbus even after they had turned off on another two-lane and began to wend their way toward a national park. Finally, we came to a crossroads in the high, cold, moonlit night. They were turning west which, in my ongoing confusion, was not my direction for now, and I regretfully said my goodbyes and stepped out of the warm and friendly spot of light into an otherwise silent plain. I stood for some time watching the tiny tail lights of that lonesome van disappear up the blacktop. Then, with a shiver, I took stock of my surroundings.

There was not much to see in the darkness... some parts of the horizon were darker than others, but perhaps most alarming, there were no headlights whatsoever within view. The cruel moon frowned downward, creating a solitary shadow on the road. I muttered to myself, zipped my jacket, and stamped my feet.

After a few minutes, I was able to make out one of those snow fences that they build to such extravagance in the West, a structure of stacked lumber well over ten feet high, but slatted, not solid, and built at a slant to help create snow drifts. This being the closest thing to shelter in sight, I made my way through the crackling weeds, pulled out my inadequate sleeping bag, and tried to settled down.

Much to my annoyance, my fingers remained numb, and my feet became distant relatives. I tried to force myself to sleep, but you can probably guess how that went. The moon fairly pried at my eyelids, such that I had no hope of sleeping and so had too much time and too much cold in my bag. I had a peculiar sense of loneliness with me, never far from my elbows, that showed up as deep sorrow that I had somehow abandoned my younger siblings to an insane asylum. Feelings of guilt and remorse coursed through me unbidden, and my blood barely squirmed. God, what a night! I could do nothing but lie there, trying to warm myself, my pathetic little gym bag as a pillow on the brittle weeds.

Slowly it washed over me that not a soul in the world, not even the nameless couple that had dropped me off, hell, not even *myself*, knew where in the world I was. Combined with the sudden remorse I felt for leaving my sisters and brothers alone, the pain almost stopped my heart. A pitiful and strangely hot tear left the outside corner of my right eye and ran ground-ward, as if to escape that cruel moon.

159

This rigor mortis went on for a painfully long time, but at last, without me even knowing it, my lights went out, and I simply awoke the next frosty morning to a shockingly bright sun. That cold sun fit me perfectly well; really, I was a little embarrassed by how I had spent the prior night, even though there was nobody there to record it. I was cold but lively and had lost all feeling of the night before; I was ready to resume my game of "hit and run" with strangers and the highway.

Chapter Forty-One
The Old Man

I was sitting on my bedroll on the side of a two-lane in northern Arizona, feeling a bit lonesome, when I wrote a note to my dad. It was God-awful quiet right there for being part of a primary road, but despite the national forest wrapping 'round, I was feeling blue. I had a tiny little pencil and my pocket-sized notebook, so the letter was a pint-sized affair.

I wrote him a nice note, thinking about him and Mother, but instead of making me feel any better, I actually felt worse. If I'd kept at it any longer, I think I'd have started to cry.

I guess the main reason I was out there in the first place was my resistance to the gravity that was my Old Man. He had a way of making everything in the world revolve around him, like everything was directed toward him and had meaning for him alone. For many years, I chalked it up to his four great battles in the Pacific... I think if I was that close to one hundred and fifty other guys, and my unit had ninety-five percent casualties, that my thinking might get kinda self-centered, too. But it was stories I heard from my uncle, Dad's brother, and their sister Coleen, that had me kinda change my mind over time... hell, he was a self-centered bastard before he enlisted! But I'm sure the war didn't help any.

I just had to break free of that constant pull... I just couldn't take being torn like that all the time. His alcoholism didn't help any either, and when he vented his frustration on me or the other kids, it was just too much. Don't get me wrong: I honor the Old Man. And I'm grateful to him for all he sacrificed, both before I was born and after. But I found over time that I could only love

161

him at a distance. It seemed like that's the only way I could love anybody.

When I look back, though, I think it's not quite right that a young man should be out crossing the country like that, on his own or with a buddy. He shouldn't be gettin' locked up in jail or have to wake up freezing beside a two-lane in the middle of nowhere. But it coulda been worse.

Really.

A lot worse.

Chapter Forty-Two

In Deep

I seemed to awaken from a stupor late that morning, realizing that the two-lane the VW bus had turned down the night before actually led to the Grand Canyon. There is a much more heavily-used road to this spectacular spot, which I ultimately used to continue my travels south, but this little road was used by more people as the day wore on. Between my inability to get a ride south and my desire to see the big hole in the ground, I decided to surrender and try for a ride to the canyon.

A very sweet pair of newlyweds picked me up, which was a bit of a surprise, and we rode all the way into the national park. Before getting to the main part of the park, we pulled over into a little wide place in the road, meant for people to sight-see. I'll never forget the moments I walked forward, and the Grand Canyon was revealed to me more and more with each step. I became silent and reverent as the grandeur of the canyon was revealed, stupefied by the sheer magnitude of the thing.

We all gabbled excitedly as we drove from pull-out to pull-out, trying to match our limited language to the magnificent terrain. We spent the rest of the day in this manner until we pulled into a campground... happily, they had reserved a spot, and we set up the spacious tent and warmed our dinner in a terrific glow. Near sunset, we raced once again to the canyon rim to experience the glorious reds and various other hues of the rock walls as the sun disappeared.

As we settled in for the evening, the male of the couple decided to go find beer. I find it surprising to this day that he would abandon his new spouse to the company of such a ragamuffin as I was, but she was as comfortable with it as he. They were generous to the extreme, pooh-poohing my protestations that I was eating and drinking too much of their kindness.

The only awkward moment came as we settled in to sleep. I had forewarned them (and they once again had pooh-poohed) that my boots were too rank to be in the same tent with us. However, once we were in our sleeping bags, the stench (to which I'd become accustomed) proved too much for my hosts, and they rather sheepishly requested that I place them outside. No problem, although I did check for scorpions in the morning.

My hosts planned a good long vacation at the park, and although I remained in awe of the natural beauty, I continued to feel the glowing ember of my mission to reach Flagstaff or Phoenix. After one more trip to the rim together, and a round of heartfelt goodbyes (including a tear from the new Missus), I once again began my trek south, this time along the much-more-heavily traveled access road.

Chapter Forty-Three
The Land of Milk and Honey

I thought I was going to find a slice of heaven in Flagstaff, and as I worked my way south, I built the story in my mind more and more. I would first crash with a friend-of-a-friend Larry, then get a job, maybe on the railroad, find an apartment, get a girlfriend hotter than Marie, and live the high life. I just knew Flag was going to be better than "Lost Wages."

I thought I had set it up beforehand, but once I walked to Larry's address, he was speechless in the doorway as I explained who I was, how our mutual friend was supposed to have talked to him, and that I was planning to sleep on his floor for a couple of weeks.

Larry had an amiable roommate Brian, but they just weren't set up for a long-term visitor. Their living room (not to mention the bedrooms) was crammed full of bachelor stuff: wood-cutting tools, a mass of fishing gear, two hunting rifles, and literally *piles* of pizza boxes and beer cartons. The front door had the tattered remnants of a stuffed sailfish arching over it, and deer heads and hooves hung on the interior walls. The primary decorations were free beer posters from the liquor store, featuring mostly-naked young women holding bottles of brew and electric smiles.

Although they graciously allowed me in, it was immediately clear that there wasn't room for a third roommate.

I set my jaw and made the best of the situation. The boys were *great* fishermen and had grilled a few trout for that afternoon. I greedily consumed all their leftovers and swilled a couple of beers. I then tried to get down to brass tacks, asking as many questions as I could about work in Flag, their work, and so on. It turned out that Larry and Brian had very good union jobs with the railroad, working shifts that left them plenty of time for fishing and other recreation. They could see that I got excited about that possibility, so they tamped me down by explaining that everyone wanted these jobs, it had taken them *years* to get on fulltime, and that although Larry would take me to the office the next day, I should not get my hopes up.

We watched TV and slowly drank beer after that, until we each crawled off to bed, mine being the lumpy, fart-smelling couch.

Down to the office we went the next morning, but the fella taking applications had a face like railroad-bed ballast: dark, stony, and unmoving. He must have handed out and taken back a hundred of these applications every week, and he was obviously weary of it. As I filled in the form, Larry took Stone Face aside to see if there was anything he could do for me. When I handed in the form, the office man looked at it quickly, forced a thin smile (though his eyes remained flinty), and said that all he had was labor work... "Do you understand what I mean?" I had no idea what he meant but said I did, and I was told to show up at "seven tomorrow, and wear your work boots!"

Larry took me home and fixed me up with an old pair of his boots, three sizes too big for me, so I stuffed paper in the toes and wore all three pairs of socks that I owned. Thank God, he also gave me an old pair of work gloves, or I never would have made it through that first day. We passed the second night very much as we had the first, including more fish and more beer, but the living room seemed to be shrinking by the hour. It was obvious that the boys didn't have girlfriends, and our behavior, bodily sounds, and level of hygiene reflected that fact.

Brian took me to work the next morning, as he was to work a shift from Flagstaff to Gallup, New Mexico. Although he was pleasant enough, I got the distinct feeling that my welcome was already wearing thin. I couldn't *wait* to get started working and make some money so I could get out on my own.

Brian dropped me off with a wry "good luck" and an odd smile. I was clumsy in my oversized boots and just clumped along to the gate I was to report to. After being admitted, I immediately sensed that something was wrong; I was the only white guy in the group. I became extremely self-conscious and began to suspect that every smile, every whispered comment in the crowd, was about me, and maybe my ridiculous boots.

Finally, a (white) foreman arrived, and we boarded an old, rough car to be taken to the worksite. After a thirty-minute ride, we all piled out: time to work. Today it was aligning the tracks on a little-used siding, and I had *no* idea of what to do. The foreman constantly barked in my direction, pointing at and mouthing the unintelligible name of some huge, exotic tool, and commanding me to get to work with it. His face was red and perspiring at all times, and the best he could do was point me toward things. I learned only by watching the black fellas, although it took me hours to understand what we were actually trying to do.

Between the glare of the boss and the sniggers of my co-workers, I had a long, uncomfortable day. As I hadn't packed a lunch, I went hungry as the others ate. Thankfully, there was a huge metal water container for the crew, so at least I had water to fill my belly.

We finished earlier than I expected, at three-thirty, then stored all the tools and piled into the odd little gang-car for the thirty-minute ride back to the yard. After punching out, I walked out to the road and stuck out my thumb; one of the white guys pulling out of the yard gave me a ride. With very few words between us, he dropped me in Larry and Brian's neighborhood and I clumped the last few blocks to their shack.

Larry was smoking pot when I stumbled in the door, and he gave me a long what-happened-to-you? face. I was crusty with sweat, and every part of my body hurt, most especially my hands. I gratefully kicked off the old boots and settled into the old couch next to Larry.

Although I had apologized profusely the night before as I ate their food and drank their beer, tonight, once Larry indicated that there was cold pizza in the tiny kitchen, I gulped down the remaining three slices and a beer while making only the most guttural of sounds.

Larry gave me a new name, "Gandy Dancer," and after watching TV with him for an hour, I simply lay down and passed out, without showering.

I lasted at the labor job for another day or two, with both my hands and feet developing blisters; but between the red-faced shouting of the foreman and the cool silence of my work-mates, I just couldn't take it anymore.

On my final day in Flagstaff, I just slept in. It happened that both Larry and Brian were aboard trains that morning, so I wrote them a nice note of thanks, guiltily consumed the last of the leftover pizza, and, leaving the work boots and gloves behind, simply hit the road.

In fact, I never did see Larry or Brian again, ever. I still owe them for that pizza and beer.

Chapter Forty-Four

Ashes to Ashes

I had to walk quite a bit that morning in Flagstaff, but I finally found my way to the two-lane heading south. I had resolved to go visit two high school buddies, Peter and Curley, who lived together in Phoenix. Phoenix: just the place to reconstruct myself from the ashes. Phoenix: I would get my bearings, find a job, and start over again.

You probably know the truth before I say it: what I actually found was a slice of still-burning hell.

I crashed with Peter and Curley for a couple of nights, and we got wild with drinking and hash brownies. I thought we were off to a good start, but in less than a week, I could feel the tension building in the little apartment. Curley got tired of me always being in the living room; Peter got tired of buying me beers; and I was taking my time finding a job.

Gradually, I began to feel "the dark" whenever I took either food or beer out of their refrigerator, but I just didn't know what to say other than what I'd already told them: "I'll be treating you guys right when I land a job."

I finally did find a job, at the Cudahy Meat Processing plant. My job, as it turned out, was at the very beginning of the cattle-slaughtering business. The slaughterhouse was a couple stories high, and my job was to get the cattle up a long series of ramps, by whatever means possible. They provided me with a prod, but I sometimes just used a broom, and I grew hoarse from screaming at the cattle all day. I don't care what anybody says, the cattle *know* what's going on in there, and they are *most*

170

reluctant to get into the chute. The company provided heavy, high rubber boots for us to wear, but I was constantly slipping in the piss-mud and shit of the yard, falling several times a day, and of course smelling to high heaven.

I also belatedly realized what an idiot I was for taking such a job in the middle of summer. I worked there for six or seven months, with the ever-present hope that the weather would cool enough to make the work less horrible, but it never did.

I gradually settled into a trance of just working all day, showering, drinking the horror of the day away, and then mercifully falling asleep only to awake and do it all over again.

I was jubilant when I received my first paycheck and gave the boys some cash for letting me sleep on their floor, making too big a deal out of bringing home some groceries and beer. Pete and Curley were glad that I was contributing, but as the months slipped by, it became clear that I was an unwanted hanger-on. The apartment was just a little too small for three people, and I wasn't earning enough to get a place of my own. Slowly the tension became palatable.

Without really meaning to, I formulated my plan. We got paid on Friday, and I took the boys out to dinner. I drank my way through another lost weekend, and on Monday morning while Peter and Curley were getting ready for work, I just moaned and rolled over. I said I wasn't feeling good, and they, fully understanding, left for work.

I finally just gathered my stuff, left my last twenty-dollar bill on their little kitchen table, and started walking to the nearest highway. Words can scarcely describe my anguish during that walk: my rage at being treated shabbily by people I thought were my friends; my sickness at finding that Phoenix *wasn't* the answer to my problems; my dry-mouth hangover from drinking too much the night before; and my mind squirming with ten thousand regrets. I was sick in my head and my stomach, the sun beat painfully into my eyes, and if I could have ended my life right then and there... that is, if God just decided to call me home, as I prayed he would, because I was too chicken-shit to take any action myself, well, then, I would have welcomed it.

I was bottomed-out in the journey-of-journeys: I had set out years ago to discover the meaning of my life, and as near as I could tell, there simply wasn't anything "out here." I had felt certain there were universal truths to be discovered, and I was sure that I would find them on my journey. Instead, I found myself desperate and alone and deeply troubled. If life back at home meant only heartache, and I hadn't found myself or my meaning "out here," what was the point of it all?

I paused in the shade of an overpass and collected myself for twenty minutes. In the end, I didn't know what else to do, other than to just push on, so that's what I did.

Chapter Forty-Five

Heading Home

I reached the point where the tires of the eighteen-wheelers no longer sang to me.

No. They took on a desultory, monotonous drone that no longer fired my imagination.

All I ever did now was "hit and run" with the occasional brief conversation broken by long periods of silence.

In parallel, the whoops and screeches of youth, fueled by alcohol and sexual desire, lost their charms. I no longer wanted to consume, to howl at the stars in mindless agony, to roar with red-faced friends over the disgusting burn of liquor. No. I gradually awoke to the fact that the life I was living was no longer for me... I had turned an invisible, half-unsuspecting corner and begun, almost without my own volition, to head toward home.

Chapter Forty-Six
Standing on a Corner

I worked my way northeast out of Phoenix via a series of short, local rides. Gradually, the saguaro gave way to thicker vegetation and then finally pine trees. I spent the night just outside of Payson, after eating a warm dinner. Although I had left my last twenty-dollar bill with Peter and Curley, I had stuffed a number of bills in different parts of my equipment, boots, socks, bag, and underwear, so that if I was robbed, I might not lose it all. I was comfortable and content in the forest outside of Payson, sensing that I was making the transition from the hellish heat of Phoenix to the more nurturing temperatures of the higher country. I had once more made a start during the springtime, so the night proved very cool, but for me this was invigorating.

Old Route 87 to Winslow is a winding affair, full of the varying beautiful vistas of Arizona. It was also a road without speed limits, so although most of my drivers were calm enough, a few were wild men who loved nothing more than to run at the highest speed possible through the twists and turns of the old highway.

I eventually pulled into Winslow in the bed of a pickup truck, in close company with a very old Navajo woman wrapped in layers of blankets and several of her grandchildren. Likewise, I caught a ride with another Navajo family, this time inside of a station wagon, from Winslow to Gallup.

I was now heading due east, even though I was not at all sure that I wanted to be heading home. But I simply had no other direction. East was as good as any other direction for now, and I kept toying with the idea of returning to my parents' home, unable to come to terms with whether or not this was the right direction.

Chapter Forty-Seven

Injun Country

The push east was a patchwork of freeways and two-lanes, as the government gradually replaced famous old Route 66 with the new Interstate 40. Apparently conceived of as a military necessity by President Eisenhower, the Interstate system was a boon to poor guys the country over, providing the fastest transport imaginable to the adventurous, free of charge.

Before I found a place to sleep, behind a church in Gallup, I wandered in wonderment down the main street. I had never seen so many Indian people before in my life, and as the evening came on, every male I saw was more-or-less disgustingly drunk. I witnessed two poor souls trying to beat each other in the middle of the street, so drunk they couldn't actually hurt one another, although one of them bled from the mouth. I cut down an alley before sunset and was shocked to find a couple engaged in a rowdy "rodeo hug" right in the middle of the alleyway... I felt so self-conscious that I simply backed out of there and found another way around. A waitress at a coffee shop suggested the church to me, and although there was a bright spotlight overhead, I found this more comforting than disturbing... I could sleep only a little that night.

In Grants, New Mexico, my driver stopped for gas and was hoodwinked by the attendant into replacing his shock absorbers. The upside for me was that the driver bought both of us lunch while we waited, a meal I badly needed.

I enjoyed the distant grandeur of Mount Taylor as I worked my way east, and my final long wait to the west of Albuquerque was at Rio Puerco, where I waited a long time. This marked the easternmost edge of the Navajo reservation for me, and I've never seen a Navajo person (that I know of) in my life since.

Not the worst of times, but that grind from Flagstaff to Albuquerque took the starch out of me, and I really needed a change. I decided to take a turn north, to the fabled land of Colorado. Although I'd been repeatedly warned by other hitchhikers that the Colorado law was hard on hitchers, I wanted to see the land. Besides, heading east still didn't sit well with me; so once again, one direction was as good as another.

Chapter Forty-Eight
Raton Pass

I enjoyed the ride into Albuquerque: all along the old highway were twenty-year-old motels, invariably shining forth a fresh coat of paint, some with pools, all with TV, and all fit for the families migrating in the opposite direct. Once in town, I swung north following old Route 6, as I'd had bad luck with a couple of rides and thought maybe things'd improve if I tried another direction. I worked my way north, getting a ride at one point from a Pueblo Indian family who seemed a bit more gregarious than my Navajo hosts had been. I slept along the road and could feel the air growing thinner and colder as I moved into higher altitude.

I spent a day in Santa Fe, which was a real pleasure: the big Catholic cathedral there; the square where a lot of Indian folks sold trinkets to white people; *lots* of real pretty older white ladies with *lots* of turquoise jewelry hanging off 'em. I actually found a Woolworth's right on the plaza and was able to buy something to eat real cheap. I slept that night along a creek that runs pretty much through the middle of town and, in the morning, started making my way back to the highway, which turned out to be a lot tougher than I expected. Don't get me wrong, the people I met were real nice, but there were a lot of older white people in very expensive cars, who, when they spotted me on the side of the road, would kind of go stony and stare straight ahead so as not to lock eyes with me. Also, out of the central part of town, the road to the main highway is a real race track, and people had a difficult time pulling over for fear of getting killed by traffic in the process. Finally, an artist-kinda fella pulled over in his beat-up pickup, and once he got a handle on my plight, drove me all the way out to I-25. He seemed to not have much money, what with his battered Chevy and raggedy clothes, but he spoke with an East-Coast accent and seemed unconcerned about the time and gas it took to run me out there. I still remember that guy, little thin goatee and mustache, black hair, a real nice guy.

Anyhow, I was able to catch rides pretty easy heading north, as there are more poor people living up that way, and the poor are always more generous to a guy than the rich, whether it's tipping you when you're waiting tables or giving you a ride. So I had a nice, unmemorable trip until I crossed the border into Colorado, and that's when I realized that perhaps the journey was beginning to wind down. I kept waffling back-and-forth about what I was doing: Stop in this town and get a job? Or go back home to Ohio? And I just kept batting it back-and-forth, unable to decide.

I stood right down on the freeway, right on Raton Pass, as traffic was very sparse, and I just didn't think the Highway Patrol would bother with such a lonesome stretch of concrete. As the sun was bright (although cool), I stood beneath the overpass, and as I was heading north, I was facing south, and I gradually came to see into my future.

Clouds were forming to the south and west that were of a most foreboding nature: black-bellied and stacked thousands of feet high. The wind began to pick up, and I began to wish I'd had something warm to eat that day. As if to provide an additional curse, a lonely car curled up the off-ramp and, much to my surprise, dropped off a blond-haired hitchhiker who, grinning all the way, stumbled down the bank to join me under the bridge. We shook hands and quickly began to opine on the weather that was headed our way. I had my usual thin jacket with me, and a hat, but little else for cold weather. My new partner offered me a plain wheat roll out of a plastic bag that he carried, and although I had to pinch off a few spots of green, I have to say I really enjoyed that roll and can remember it to this day, perfectly round on the bottom, with a kind of wave on top, buttery!

Although fed, my gut started to clench up as the clouds moved in on us, and my mind was stunned that the weather could turn so foul so fast. My new sidekick had fair skin, and his cheeks glowed from the steady, sheering wind, which grew colder by the moment. In the long lulls between cars, we took to hugging our own selves with our hands underneath our armpits, trying to cheer each other with little quips ("this has *got* to be a freak storm!"), but both knowing that a night out here beside the road was going to be very long and painful.

The sun dropped behind the clouds, and although it was a little time until sundown, I swear the temperature dropped ten degrees. I started to get real worried... I couldn't see any comfortable options in my future. Gradually the sky grayed, and the feeling of a very early nightfall began to cloak us.

As I was turned within, blackly contemplating my few options, not one but two huge tanker trucks began to pull over, squeaking and gasping as the huge airbrakes took hold, the engines grumbling loudly as they were downshifted. They stood panting and waiting, and so I climbed into the first one, and Fair Hair climbed into the second. I was giddy with relief and had a sense that a minor miracle was happening. The cab was over-warm, if anything, and of course windless, and I felt delivered into a safe haven. We began rolling north, and it wasn't thirty minutes too soon because flakes of snow began to twirl in front of the windshield. My mind still could not accept that this was actually snow... I hadn't seen it since leaving back East so long ago.

Our hosts were hauling tankers of jet fuel to an Air Force facility in Colorado Springs, and my driver was the nicest fella. Of course, he was a little rough around the edges, but his command of creative cursing was something to behold. On the other hand, I was no sophisticate myself, looking and smelling as I did from many a day out in the open air since Phoenix. We talked, I asked polite questions about his rig, and I might have overdone it on thanking him for picking me up... I was just so grateful. We listened to the chatter on the CB radio, and although the snow kept increasing, we didn't give it a lot of thought for a half-hour or so. In that short time, the sky turned utterly black, and the world felt like midnight, although it couldn't have been past seven o'clock.

Increasingly, we became concerned... the snow fell so thick that the wipers could barely keep up, and the snow wasn't melting off the road anymore... it was thick and, as my driver said, "slicker than owl snot." I kept leaning forward to look in the right-hand mirror, to see if our companions were keeping up... I could see the haze of their headlights, and that was about all.

Now, it's probably seventy-five miles more or less from Raton Pass to Colorado City on I-25, but the weather clenched us like a boa constrictor, restricting our sight, our road, our world, and it seemed like our very air, until there was nothing but a small black hole ahead of us. My driver, tense as any driver I've ever seen, kept us boring into that black tunnel at an ever-slower rate. Every few minutes, he would drop down another gear,

181

sometimes using the rear differential shifter, pushing as hard as he could without getting us killed.

We got off the road at Colorado City, real slow and careful like, me mindful of the explosive load in the tanker six feet behind us, and crawled toward the vague lights of a motel-restaurant along the frontage road. It didn't take long to figure out that there were no rooms here, nor anywhere else for that matter, and my guy, who by all appearances was the more experienced and better driver, determined that we should push on.

In an agonizing endorsement of my judgment, we soon heard a shout over the CB radio from the other truck... before we even got off the frontage road, Fair Hair and the other driver had slid sideways into a ditch and desperately called for us to return. Slowly, carefully, my driver brought his monster around, passed the stuck rig, made a second U-turn, and then pulled up very tight to the cab of the second truck... if I cared to reach into the frigid air, I could have touched the driver's side mirror on the other cab.

We all dismounted, and although the other hitchhiker and I were of no use, we stood resolutely at hand, the flakes swirling thick around us, helping with the chain as we could. We got the tail end of the first truck hitched to the front end of the second, and gladly did I run back and hop into the first cab, as my arms were shivering uncontrollably.

I have to confess that I really didn't think this tow job would work... I half expected to feel my/our rig slide sideways to join the other in the ditch. I had to sit as far back in my seat as possible, to allow my driver to observe the goings-on at the rear of our tanker, and was gleefully surprised when I saw him smile as our cab inched forward... slowly, slowly we pulled forward until all parts of our ninety-foot, three-jointed beast had all thirty-six feet planted on pavement.

Once more into the black and the swirling flakes, then Fair Hair and I stood by while the drivers disengaged the beasts. There was no point in us boys standing there like that, but our dedication to our drivers was such that we'd endure any hardship if it meant that we could lend a hand. Finally, with chains and gloves stowed, we all mounted up again and crawled away from the lights, back into the emptiness of the highway.

My driver shared a little coffee with me, and I think a little food, but he had really only packed for himself, so I was careful not to take much of anything... he had given me so much already. We found our way down the on-ramp and onto the deserted interstate, moving with great care, the mirrors on the cab shuddering in the wind at times. The dozens of pale blue lights on the dashboard glowed calmly through the storm and lit up my host's face in a most heroic way.

We toiled like this, in our tiny universe, for what seemed like hours.

Finally, very late at night, and with the snow swirling uninterrupted, a rest- stop sign hove into sight, glowing green in the headlights, and my driver did the sensible thing which was to pull over. The second truck followed us, and gratefully, we all shut down. My driver went through a mental checklist, shutting down this and not that, until the truck showed parking lights, and idled calmly and quietly in the silence of the snow. He actually got down (although I didn't join him) to check on the other driver and then climbed back up. He was apologetic that he was taking the sleeping compartment for himself, but it was nothing to me... the thin, vinyl-covered mat looked filthy and dusty to me, and I was in a warm padded seat in the eye of a blizzard, so it was no-never-mind to me. My driver looked haggard, even in the thin blue lights of the dashboard, and it seems to me that no sooner could I smell that his were boots off than he began to roar with sleep. I more passed out than slept, and brother, I don't know how many hours I was like that, but it was a pitch-black and dreamless sleep that night.

I awoke with a start and a very stiff neck. My driver already had his boots on and was kind of wiggling down into his seat. He looked a lot better, and you wouldn't believe it, but it was a crystal clear morning, the sun glowing red and right through my window, the sky a Waterford bowl. Out of context, a freight train, with bright yellow and red engines, moved easily down the tracks to our right in contrast to our immobility. My driver seemed in good spirits, though, and he shrugged on his coat, and jumped down to check on the other tanker. We all ran through the cold, which got all of us bright-eyed, to use the rest-stop toilet, and then with smiles and winks we all climbed aboard to continue the journey.

Behemoth One ground forward in a loop around the toilets, and then we were surprised to see the other rig not moving. Then we could see it moving, only with a shuddering side-step, like Behemoth Two was wounded. My guy looped back again, and we went through the ritual of hooking up (Fair Hair and me standing there stupidly in the cold) and gave number two a tug, but strangely, despite the very flat parking lot, the second tanker just slid around... it simply couldn't get its footing. Great, loud, and very creative cussing ensued. Banging of tires with metal rods, along with various kicking, left us pretty much where we started. I can only assume that truck number two had the wrong kind of tires on or something. A certain tension arose between the two drivers; and between the fatigue and frustration, the bright morning took on an unhappy flavor. At one point, the two of us boys clambered into the sleeping berth of the first rig (indeed a dusty affair) and the second driver got in the passenger seat. But as we looped around to pull back out toward the highway, the second driver decided he was going to stay with his rig, in hopes that the sun would improve his footing. He climbed down, and my guess is he did it to get away from the stewing of my driver.

Surprisingly, my hitchhiking partner immediately started squirming down to the passenger seat. Although I had a brief flash of anger (thinking he wanted the seat), he very quickly made his goodbyes to the two of us. I stammered out a quick "c'mon" but he was resolute, and with a brief "no, I'm staying with him," the door slammed and I never saw him again.

My driver and I began our slow roll north, the morning a spectacle of clean white, the frozen crystals a constant shimmer in the morning light. His forehead looked like a thunderhead for a half hour or so, but he gradually relaxed and began to enjoy himself again. There was some traffic on the road now… the plow trucks had been through during the night, and although it was still quite cold, the traffic made the lanes visible and drivable. Nothing a freight hauler likes better than to be just rolling along.

Before I climbed down in Colorado Springs, I said a very warm and sincere "goodbye" and "thank you" to my driver… I never did get his name. I felt that we had shared something of an adventure together. But it was more than that. I genuinely liked the man. I felt a small grief in my throat as he pulled away. I could feel my insides warming up to humanity. I felt a genuine desire to be with others, at least for a while, at least for longer than a two-hundred-mile ride. This had gravity for me.

Like I said, I could feel my journey turning, turning, and for the first time, I could conceive of it coming to an end. I remained ambivalent: "Should I or shouldn't I?" But the events of the previous night had made a great impression on me: the great beasts coupling and uncoupling; the people caring so much for one another in the midst of misery; Fair Hair's loyalty to his new friend. All of this began to sink into me, to leave me desirous of connection, of family, of friends, and, dare I say it? of home.

Chapter Forty-Nine

Coyote

I had encountered coyotes a couple of times in the Southwest desert... the first time I had a start, as I perceived a wild animal circling around me, albeit at a distance. Then I laughed to see how alike we were: his coat a match to my dirty tan, the two of us hot and tired in the endless sun. He looked like he had eaten even less than I had in the last two days.

I kept reassuring myself that coyotes *never* attack humans and planning how I might defend myself with rocks and all. I had plenty of time on my hands on that particular two-lane, as the traffic was lighter than light, so my mind began to toy with thoughts of rabid animals ganging up on me. I got more and more jumpy, seeing coyotes glaring at me from behind every bush in the flat landscape. I wished for more cars to roll by. But my perception may have been mistaken, and gradually the sandy coat of that solitary song-dog simply disappeared into the background.

The second was a brief encounter with a similar animal, again, out in the middle of nowhere: the coyote trotted across the still-cool asphalt so near that I could hear his nails clicking on the hard surface. Again, I started, but he was gone in an instant... unbelievable that an animal of that size could disappear so completely, so quickly, with me looking after him with interest.

Now, my growing-up years were filled with nightmares, most of them for very weak reasons: a movie about Johnny Appleseed; one about an Irish leprechaun; and even one about Davy Crockett had all brought me screaming and sweating to the middle of the night. But for me, the one dream that haunted me all my life was that of dogs. Before I learned of how canines kill their prey, I'd already had a hundred shuddering visions of my throat being ripped out by a snarling dog, with me screaming and thrashing about. So it was no surprise to me that I was on the nervous side regarding wild dogs.

I became more accustomed to the *sound* of coyotes in my time in the West, as one can hear them yipping or wailing their way through the night. I won't bore you with the details, but I can tell you that lying alone in the dark, without a fire, and listening to that mournful yowling can make a body feel as lonely as any sound on earth.

The third encounter came soon after the ride with the truck drivers in Colorado. That first blast of winter was quickly warmed away, and emboldened by the balmy weather, I decided to have a look around the High Country. I was still arguing with myself about whether or not I was really headed home, and my ambivalence about where to go and what to do was so strong that I took one last stab at *not* following my heart. I ate a big, warm breakfast in Colorado Springs, and after considering various options, I decided to take one more stab at independence... I had heard that a big mine up near Leadville was hiring, and I found the idea of living in the "highest incorporated city in North America" too romantic to pass up. I of course wanted to visit Denver, the home of Neil Cassady and Jack Kerouac, but the idea of working in a mine kept pecking at my eggshell mind, begging to be born. Although I had passed through a terrific storm the night prior, I decided to head west again, to give myself one last chance at striking the mother lode.

188

I headed out of from Colorado Springs, up around fabled Pike's Peak, across a high plain called "South Park," and up into the snow-covered mountains beyond. The rides themselves are unmemorable, but the scenery has remained fixed in my mind all these years.

That land up above ten-thousand feet is another world altogether. Summer never really reaches that high; I was stunned to find how cold it was in the very early fall, with me just coming up from the warmth of New Mexico. It takes a different kind of person to live up at that altitude, I can tell you from a few of those rides... one fella worked at the huge mine up there outside of Leadville; he picked me up very early one sparkling morning, with a tall boy of beer between his thighs already... whew! He drove a beat-up pickup and was heading to Buena Vista for eggs. I asked him about the quality of the eggs, why he was driving so far, but he didn't have much to share on the subject. I realized much later that a break from the family was more the heart of the matter. The things of value he *did* share with me were: a) the mine wasn't hiring at that particular time, b) there was no housing within one hundred miles of the mine, and c) if I didn't have transport, I might as well forget it.

Anyway, back to the coyotes. I camped one night near Leadville, in a forested area near a few homes. I walked back to the edge of town to a grocery store and bought myself some decent food, because that cool weather can make you feel most empty. This was after sunset, and I was surprised at how dark it was when I came out of the store.

I was walking back toward my cold camp, a little uncertain as to whether or not I was in the right copse of woods, when I happened to notice a little movement out of the corner of my eye. In the gloom, I thought my eyes were playing tricks on me as, although I jerked quickly to the right, I saw nothing. My nerves came on end though and as I continued to walk, I felt that my every step was gunshot-loud; I was conscious of how I stumbled along toward my pitiful home: a sleeping bag and a small gym bag.

The next time I glanced to my right, I could see the dark shadow of the coyote as he stood watching me in the faint light... he seemed neither aggressive nor frightened, only watchful. I stared long and hard and then resumed my march through the high, now-dead weeds, toward what I believed was my destination.

I glanced to the right, and my heart fairly stopped. The coyote was keeping pace with me about twenty yards away.

I stopped, and so did he.

I worked to calm myself, which I badly needed. He again stood coolly staring at me, and so I turned back to my trudging. In an instant, I was frozen again: this time by the sight of not one, but two dark figures racing across the dim trail ahead of me. I began to pant audibly and questioned my own sanity. When I finally relocated my first "shadow," sure enough, there were now three, not just one or two, across the gray-looking grass. I began to feel my sanity slip.

I tried to split my vision, one eyeball on the little trail leading toward my camp and the other over my right shoulder, trying to keep my tormentors in sight. But I could not do both and soon lost sight of both. I again stopped and calmed myself, searching about for a landmark with which to orient myself. My breath caught in my throat then, as I saw the three of them the same distance from me as before, calmly observing me, the one in front of the other two, but no closer (nor any farther) than before.

By luck, I saw the three pine trees in a clump that I had memorized prior to the stroll to the store and made toward them in haste. I no longer tried to look in two directions at once but did keep my head rolling about, looking every which way as I walked quickly. Suddenly, I stopped again. This time, in addition to the three on my right, I now had two coyotes on my left, *five*! I was beside myself with anxiety and rushed to my pathetic camp.

As I scrambled to roll my things together, dropping and packing and rolling all at once, I noticed again how all of the canines kept a constant distance from me. I had the distinct feeling of being tracked by these animals, a feeling unique in my experience, and this feeling gave way to a pronounced thrill within me.

As I said, I was camped near a little neighborhood with a street and all, and I longed to be surrounded by the comfort of these homes. I made straightaway toward a little alleyway between two of the houses, bordered on both sides by fencing, a nice little gap back into society. I almost broke into a run as I neared the little alley, but once at the mouth of the gap, I suddenly wheeled around to face my demons. There they all were, still about twenty yards away, still keeping track of me, still calm and unaggressive. But I simply could not turn my back on them again. I slowly, slowly backed my way down the little bordered gap, watching, ever watching those coyotes, who remained frozen where they were in the wild as I gradually returned to civilization.

In the end, I never actually feared for my life, only my sanity. Those shadowy creatures were simply impassively observing me. It was my reaction to them that made such a stir within me. It was the old nightmares of the dogs at my throat that caused me to rush as I did. As my breath settled down, I gradually came to realize that it was time, in so many ways, for me to work my way back to friends and family. I reflected long on my time with the jet-fuel haulers down on the Front Range: how we had struggled together and endured hardship together; how the trucks had become joined as one, then separated again, then joined and separated again. All of this grew in me in a way which caused my inside world to match my outside world.

I had experienced the highest country that I would ever sleep in, and now I was heading down.

Chapter Fifty

Final Mirage

Heading east out of Leadville sounds a little easier than it was. Early in the morning, there was a huge rush of vehicles northeast as workers tried to get to the big molybdenum mine on time, but from there on, the traffic was very thin. What later became the huge resort of Copper Mountain was a fly speck on the map then. So it was a slow, lonely, cold morning which finally gave way to a bit of traffic heading to Summit County, where (I was informed) there was an actual supermarket.

Rather than take Eisenhower Tunnel under the Continental Divide, I found myself winding and winding, ever higher, over Loveland Pass on Route 6, the very route my hero Kerouac had used to traverse the country. Once over the pass, I rolled all the way to Denver in only a few rides, fascinated to find the Larimer Street of Dean Moriarty's youth.

I had the good fortune to land a ride close to the downtown district and eagerly began to scan the streets and buildings for some sign of "he-who-went-before." It was late afternoon, though, so I didn't find what I was looking for. I began to cast about for where I might sleep but, frankly, the street bums there looked tougher and meaner than any I'd encountered along the way... I think they were putting on their armor for colder weather. I abandoned my plans to sleep near Cherry Creek and kept walking until I found (surprise!) a dark spot right in a large park in the middle of the city. (I won't even tell you where, as I might want to use that spot again someday.) I slept fitfully, as if one eye was always open, but no one including the cops came near where I was, so I did manage to get some sleep.

I awoke with a sense of dedication, that I should find something in Denver to fit the puzzle, to answer at least part of the riddle, and so I hid my gear where I'd slept and trudged around the noisy downtown, looking for clues.

Denver was enjoying one of those fabulous autumn days that often come after the first snowfall: warm, sunny, and very clear. My shoulders dropped a full two inches as I relaxed in the warmth.

In contrast to the brilliant weather, my explorations grew darker. The streets in Denver are confusing as they don't run parallel, and I finally had to stop a couple of locals to ask for directions, folks who gave terse responses and hurried away. I finally found my way to the neighborhood of Neil's youth and had my final letdown of this long journey: the place was a run-down, dangerous, long-neglected corner of the downtown area, with no redeeming qualities that I could fathom. By noon, I was badly dejected and thought it best to treat myself to a sandwich and a beer or three.

The bar was cool and dim, but not intimidating in the least. There were only a few customers, and the bartender-waiter was a very friendly fella. After my sandwich, I moved to the bar for another beer and to pump the man for information. I was soon shocked to find that not only did he know who Jack Kerouac was, but he had actually served him, many a time, at this very bar. I was speechless for some time.

The man didn't volunteer much, so I had to finally pull myself together and ask, "Well, what was he like?"

"What was who like?"

194

"Jack Kerouac, a course!" I felt a little embarrassed.

"Well…" The barman, who was a bit older, looked at me carefully and paused before continuing.

"I occasionally have folks ask me about that." He paused again and then began to slowly wipe down the bar. "Jack couldn't hold his liquor, see… so he wasn't my favorite customer, if you understand my meaning."

I was confused and again speechless. I felt that I'd lost my compass points. I was unsure what to ask next.

"But did you enjoy talking to him? Did you learn anything from him?" I'm afraid that I sounded desperate.

The bartender barked a short laugh, and continued putzing around the back bar. "Oh, he was okay to talk to, but no, I never learned anything from him!" He smiled silently, nearly smirking into the mirror over the back bar. "No, sir."

I soon stumbled back out into the bright afternoon as confused and aimless as a newborn. I felt sick, and half-drunk, and half-blind, and utterly lost. My only direction was back toward the park and my sparse belongings.

I just kind of hung around there all day, walking to a convenience store when I wanted a beer and trying to come to grips with the emptiness I felt within. The clear, beautiful day was no comfort to me; but in the evening, my dark corner of the park let me feel more secure, and I fell asleep early.

My vagabond world utterly deflated, I began my trek east out of Denver, away from the mountains, and out of the West of my imagination. All was disappointment, all was illusion, all was despair. All this travel, all this hunger, all this terrible effort, and I had found nothing. Nothing to inform my life, to give me meaning, to provide a universal truth. There was just me, and the wind, and the highway, and plains as far as the eye could see...

Chapter Fifty-One
Straight, Flat, and Dry

My mind was so filled with defeat, disappointment, and loss that I remember little about my rides out of Denver headed east. The little I do recall was like my entrance to Montana headed west, many years ago: the snowcapped peaks, like clouds, receding into the distance, as I was gradually enveloped by the plains of eastern Colorado. After a brilliant morning-show of red and yellow clouds, I continued my plod homeward, still not sure that I was doing the right thing. But behind me were only shattered illusions. As Gertrude Stein famously said: "There's no 'there' there." I had given it all I had, but there was nothing left for me in Oregon, California, Nevada, Arizona, New Mexico, or Colorado. All the destinations of my dreams were now dust; I just couldn't come up with any option other than to head home and make the best of the situation.

Across the great state of Kansas I flew, the rides long only because there are such great distances between towns. In the late fall weather, the fields looked lifeless, brittle, and gray. My state of mind matched the pitiful, fallow fields.

I experienced one great pulsation in Hays, Kansas. An older male driver, with an accomplice up front with him, stopped to pick me up. I could smell the alcohol in the car, even as I queried through the passenger window as to where they were headed. Since cities like Hays present an obstacle to hitchhiking, I was very glad that they were going all the way through to the eastern suburbs. I climbed in the back, where a nervous-looking, thin young man, obviously the son of the driver, sat next to me. The amusement park ride began almost immediately, as the driver wove furiously across the lanes, oblivious to oncoming traffic. I began to paw around for a seat belt, but try as I might, could not put my hands on one. I felt as vulnerable as the proverbial canary with the cat waiting outside the cage. The weaving continued unabated for miles, with me coughing up the occasional warning sound, and the silent son simply pounding on the front seat whenever collision seemed inevitable.

We made it through Hays unscathed, which remains a miracle in my mind, and I finally got out forty-five minutes later, deeply shaken. I didn't even flag cars for ten minutes or so, as I caught my breath and reviewed my own cowardice: I should have refused the ride when I smelled the alcohol, or I should have demanded that they let me out, something other than silently holding my breath as death sheared close over and over again. But I saw myself in that silent boy, unable to speak a word, rather wordlessly pounding on the front seat, trying to get the old man's attention.

What would going home be for me, I wondered? Should I become wordless again? Yet I was set on the course eastward, and I could think of no other destination.

Chapter Fifty-Two
Lessons from the Heart-Land

After the heart-pounding experience in Hays, I soon found myself hunkered down at the side of the highway, surveying my prospects. I felt unnaturally old and tired, the effect of too many days on the road. I was plunked down in farmland, with little to entertain the eye on an autumn afternoon. I reviewed my journey from the early days until now: my early, bright-eyed enthusiasm; my many adventures with long-lost friend Michael; my outrageous experiments in San Francisco; the love and hard work in Las Vegas; and of late, the endless wandering, looking for something that remained elusive to me.

I had set out with such confidence: in the great, mythical West, I would find myself, find universal truth, become a man, and never look back. Yet here I sat on my dirty sleeping bag, headed back to whence I had come: no richer, no smarter, no happier, and certainly no wiser. What was the meaning of all this? I simply had no answer... there was no answer.

Actually, there was one answer, the one which I at first refused to consider, like the impassive coyote, fleeting in the corner of my eye, something I dreaded to face head-on. That answer was: "Nothing."

At first I felt myself go flat... the thought of "nothing" sent a cool fear through my frame, but I soon allowed myself to drift deeper into the possibility. I began to surrender my quest for a universal truth... I hadn't found one, anyway, and I toyed more and more with the possibility that it all depended on where and when one is born: To what church did one's parents belong? In what small town or big city did I take pride in living? How did I identify with the sports team/school/state/country? All this earthly activity, identification, foundation, projection: Could it all be just a fabrication? Could it all be but a house of cards, ready to fall at the first breeze? I toyed and toyed with the possibilities as I sat at the roadside, awaiting my next ride.

As I sat and allowed that "nothing" to fill me, a great deep wail grew from within me and emerged, unbidden, into the stark landscape. I wept uncontrollably, oblivious to the few cars that passed, the wail reverberating through me again and again until I could feel no more. I was empty.

Finally, I stood up, wiped my eyes with a cold wrist, and stuck out my thumb.

The second lesson from Kansas was of an entirely different nature. Two black men picked me up after dark, on the west side of Kansas City, and we barreled toward the city center, with the radio and the front-seat passenger bellowing at top volume. Both were obviously drunk, but just as in Hays, I found myself unable to insist that they let me out... I said a pitiful prayer and just hoped that we'd all survive the ride. As we neared central Kansas City, the passenger turned toward me in the back and, still bellowing, insisted that he was "Big John" and that if I had trouble with anybody in Kansas City, all I needed to do was say that I was friends with Big John, and that no one would bother me after that.

As we curled down the exit ramp to an inner-city boulevard, there was an awkward minute as the two men intended to take me downtown with them, but I insisted that I wanted to stay on the freeway and keep heading east. They seemed to think I was crazy, as it was Saturday night, but finally pulled over and let me pile out. The last I heard as the car muttered away from me was

Big John still giving me encouragement, in case I had any trouble.

Indeed, I did think I had trouble, as I wasn't about to try to settle down to sleep in the neighborhood I was in, and I felt forlorn about the possibility of getting a ride. To my shock, a white man pulled over within ten minutes and drove me well into Missouri.

But it's Big John that stays with me: his confidence, his magnanimity, his insistence on his central role in the world around him... he had found a way to define the meaning of his life, and right or wrong, living or dead, he bellowed into the nighttime full sure of his role. I've never needed to say to anyone that "I know Big John," but I keep that in my hip pocket at all times, just in case.

Chapter Fifty-Three

Stah(r)

Hitching across the middle of the country comes in fits and starts. You might get a ride for one whole exit, but the fella feels like he's doing you a big favor, or you might get a ride that'll take you across three states. Long after dark on a cold autumn night, I caught a ride in Missouri with a green van, no side windows. Within were a blond, long-haired man and his very lean, edgy Doberman Pincer. The dog scared me for a minute, until my host calmed her with just a few words. I was really happy to find out he was cutting way east toward New Jersey, so we were in for a long ride together.

After we got rolling, he grilled me for a couple of minutes in a surprisingly personal way. Between the man's questions and the dog, I got to feeling a bit queasy, but his intent was soon revealed. He pointed his right thumb to the back of the van, which (aside from the usual piles of sleeping and storage junk) included any number of huge hands of marijuana, hung to dry. He was burning across the country from California to New Jersey, and after the pot had dried, he'd sell it to finance his trip. He was also packing a case of Coors beer in between the front seats, and as he already had one tucked between his legs, he offered me one.

"Dope will get you through times of no friends, better than friends will get you through times of no dope!" he declared.

My blond-mane host regaled me with stories of his hard life in Jersey, culminating in how he and his friends had kicked out the eyes of a bar owner who had offended them. To this day, I feel like that particular story was meant as a warning. He also told me for the first time in my life about "curbing," a practice so savage that I won't relay the details here, but you can guess that it gave me a chill.

Once the dog was settled down, I began to appreciate her beauty. Blond Man related that her name was "Stah." (For anyone outside of New Jersey, it would be "Star.") She was named for the white markings on her reddish forehead. Despite my earlier brushes with the law, we happily smoked pot and sipped sixteen-ounce cans of beer as we sped eastward.

We rolled along comfortably for many a mile, and I began to have fantasies of closing the loop of my travels, as he was intent on a straight burn to the East Coast. However, a snag in my plans began to appear as I drank my fourth tall boy... he was expecting me to drive through the night... he wasn't just giving me a ride, he saw me as a tool to help him get home faster. He drove at a constant, furious pace (surprising when you consider the drugs and alcohol in the van), stopping only long enough to empty one tank and fill another. I learned to pee thoroughly during any break in the action. The man was hell-bent on getting back to Jersey. The knowing that I was to disappoint this man began as a tough walnut in my low gut and continued to increase in size as evening began to envelop us.

Right at sundown, we experienced one of the strangest spectacles of my drifting life. To this day, I don't have an explanation for it, but suddenly, large insects began to strike the windshield. At first this was just odd, but not a problem... but things went from odd to dangerous as the windshield became a Rorschach of yellow goo. My driver struggled to continue, weaving and bobbing his head to see between the blotches, but the torrent increased to a noisome staccato. He started the windshield wipers, pulling furiously at the washer lever, and the goo thickened, a great mess of wings and legs bunching under the wiper blades; the glass became unusable. I thought of rolling down a window to peer out but realized we'd just have the bugs in the van with us, so I sat clenching my entire body, waiting for what was next. I was terrified that he would continue his mad pace, but despite his furor, he began to slow and come to terms with his defeat by insects. The great thing is that his crazy speed-induced pace may have been a blessing to us. Soon after we slowed to a crawl, with the driver continuing to search for peepholes through the mess, we drove out of the swarm. The lights of a gas station beckoned us in for a stop, where I took care of my first priority at the men's room around back, but by the time I returned, he was impatiently waiting, engine running, wanting to get back on the road. The windshield, though hardly what one would call clean, was clear enough to allow us to launch, and so the green meteor once again roared into the night.

The driver finally got groggy enough from the pot and the beer that he pulled over and had me take the wheel. He climbed in the back with Star, and soon the two of them were off to Jersey in their minds, legs twitching and low moans escaping their lips.

I tried every trick I knew to keep moving east: switching positions in the seat; driving with my left foot on the gas; head back so as to look through little slits; head forward to look through eyes wide open; even pinching and slapping myself... I rolled on until I knew I was a danger... I actually woke up, not once, but twice, doing sixty-five miles an hour, and that's when I finally decided that enough was enough.

I glanced back at the duo asleep in the back, and they seemed deep and far away. I pulled off at the next exit and tried to keep the swerving and bumping to a minimum. They stayed dead asleep until I finally came to a stop. I shut off the van and leaned back in the seat, planning to nap for just a while and then start up again.

The moment the engine went quiet, Blond Man was up and angry: "What's going on?!" I tried to explain that I needed some shuteye before we continued, but he was immediately up beside me in the van, disgustedly jerking his thumb for me to get in the rear while he drove. I would guess it was two a.m. by this time.

I crawled to the back, hoping to actually get some sleep, but the dog was in as foul a mood as her owner... she intermittently growled deep in her throat and kept getting up and shifting around, all the while glaring at me... I was too nervous to sleep by this time.

Unable to sleep, I watched the road signs from the back of the van. The tension was darker than the gloom we had melted through. I began to spin my lie about a buddy I had decided to go visit and that I would get out at the intersection with I-55. I finally parted company with the East Coast all-stars and heaved a sigh of relief. Although I kept chiding myself about losing such a long-distance haul, I knew I'd never be able to stand the tension between me and them for the duration. I realized that I just couldn't take it any more: the drinking, the weed, and then whatever drugs others (like my driver in the green van) were taking... I was just sick of the whole scene, getting too old for it, you might say. I was sick and tired of being sick and tired.

It's unfair of me to pass judgment, as the very act of hitchhiking is, in a way, using others. But to be seen by that blond driver as a tool, to be used to accomplish his own ends, has chapped me ever since.

It's better to do things out of love rather than utility.

Chapter Fifty-Four
The Promised Land, Part Two

Just east of St. Louis, I-55 connects northern and southern Illinois. I spent a fitful night in a very loud and not very dark patch of grass right at the intersection of I-70 and 55, and I awoke groggy, hungry, disheveled, and disoriented. I stumbled toward the highway, with my stomach gripping and aching.

Standing along the road, calm, clean, and well-fed, was another hitchhiker. As I approached him, he smiled broadly, a very generous gesture considering that I was possible competition for a ride. Indeed, his smile fairly gleaned, matched only by the sun rising behind him. My new companion, slight and athletic, sported a short "afro" although very fair-skinned, and the sun shone through his hair like a halo. Francis (Frank) O'Herlihy welcomed me into his life that morning, and we have remained friends ever since. He was so welcoming to me that day, and so he has ever remained. I must have misunderstood his last name that morning, as I've always called him "Harley" (as in "Harley ever starts"), and he's never objected.

Frank took one look at me and immediately opened his duffel bag, extracting what food he had left: two slightly moldy bagels. I was, honestly, *too* eager to share in Harley's meager supplies and gulped down one-and-a-half of the bagels before I caught my breath, then passed the plastic bag back to him. My new friend was traveling to Akron, Ohio, to connect with a group of spiritual seekers he had heard about. Thus we would be traveling together for quite a long distance. Although I had just gotten off I-70 the night before, I was now back on the same path. We communed on his bread that morning and have broken bread together many evenings since. For me, he was, and remains, a lifesaver.

I don't know if it was Harley's little afro or not, but a black man stopped for us, which was a bit unusual, and this ride proved to be a remarkable one. The driver was exhausted from driving all night, and all he wanted from us was to keep him moving east on I-70. After the previous night fraught with intimidation, implied violence, an angry dog, and almost no sleep, I might easily have felt resentful toward another request to be of utility to a driver headed east. But I found myself entirely caring for our new driver; he was gentle, kind, and actually *asked for* rather than demanded our help. I realized then that the context of being of assistance was more important to me than whether or not I helped someone.

So we got in the front, and our driver climbed into the back and immediately fell into a deep sleep. Harley, radiant, alert, and eager, drove while I nodded off over and over in the passenger seat. And so we rolled eastward hour after hour. Our host was a very generous and friendly companion, only too happy to awaken every few hours to fuel the car... he even bought us a meal (and a pile of snacks) along the way. I don't recall why this man was pushing so hard to get where he was going, but for Harley and me, he was a blessing.

After eight or so hours, we rolled into Columbus, Ohio, which is where Francis and I were to turn north toward Akron and Cleveland. The black man, ever friendly and thankful to us, was refreshed enough to take back his grueling drive... he even left us with a brown bag of the picked-through snacks to sustain us for the day.

The weather had turned as we traveled east, and a bitter wind now scoured the landscape on this late autumn afternoon. The sky was overcast from horizon to horizon, and I was soon wearing every piece of clothing that I owned. Harley seemed comfortable enough throughout our brief travels north, a constant grin on his face, whereas I was constantly hunkered into my light jacket, shivering and resentful. I doubt that an Ohio driver would have picked *me* up, but they seemed delighted to receive Frank's warm personality into their rolling homes.

We arrived in Akron before I knew it.

Chapter Fifty-Five

The Secret of Life

I was initially very nervous about meeting the spiritual group that lay at the end of Harley's quest. I had long before drifted away from the church of my parents, and I had met enough "Jesus Freaks" along the way that I didn't want any more of the fundamentalist view of the here nor the hereafter. Francis was entirely nonchalant about my participation, welcoming me to come or not as I felt guided.

Once in Akron, we found a pay phone where Harley called his associates. As the sun was setting, and the air biting, I thought it best to at least give the spiritual group one night. Two older gents soon picked us up from beneath the lights of a gas station where we'd agreed to meet, and they took us to a meeting of the group in someone's front room.

It is difficult to describe my astonishment at this odd gathering of normal-looking folks, both men and women, all of them dressed in their work clothes, some in greasy overalls, some in ties and jackets, the women in pantsuits. This was the loudest, most profane, most blasphemous spiritual group imaginable, and I instantly fell in step. The hour-long meeting was followed by small clutches of men and women talking constantly, and a rolling laughter echoed throughout the house all evening. I don't believe I've ever seen more coffee consumed at a spiritual meeting in my life.

Francis and I spent weeks in Akron, among the most remarkable of my life. They put us to work, Harley in a retail shop and me in a grocery store, mostly handling boxes and inventory, and in this way we earned our keep plus a few dollars for spending.

(One of the members put us up every night for the two weeks.) What was extraordinary about these folks is that they didn't use alcohol or drugs, yet they seemed to be the happiest people I'd ever encountered. They didn't press their spirituality on me, nor did they hide it: how they lived their lives was in plain sight, for me to pick up or not.

So here it was, provided to me in someone's front room, no more than thirty miles from where I had been born: the Secret of Life. And all I had to do, if I wanted it, was to pick it up. I had traveled thousands of miles, searching in so many exotic places, remaining hungry in so many ways for such a long time, and here was the answer to my question, in a middle-class home, with middle-class people, in a middle-class town south of Cleveland.

And here is the Secret of Life for you, if you will have it, with a short prelude:

My thoughts beside the road in Kansas were indeed true after all: there really is no meaning for my life and no universal truth for any of us "out there." I had dreamed that the vaguely-defined West would provide me with what I needed within, but this was all mirage... the secret had lain within all this time, and it was my duty, my task, my obligation, to open the secret myself. The meaning for my life is the meaning I give to my life, in this way: it is of no use to dream of a perfect life or to wish that my life was different in some way. The secret to life is to simply accept what has been given me, what cards have been dealt to me, and to do the best I can with those. Once I accepted this simple, stark fact, I haven't had a drink or drug, because I stopped wanting to be anywhere else other than right here, right now. I've learned how to live life, on life's terms. This life has plenty of excitement and drama and entertainment for me (or for anyone), and so each day I try to just live according to this basic spiritual principle. I remain profane and blasphemous and very, very happy, to this day.

Chapter Fifty-Six
End of the Road

Akron is not so very far from Cleveland, and months ago I had started drifting back home. So now, although it was December, I began the last leg of my long journey. As I humped a pack to the highway, the snowflakes swirled, dotting my hair and face until I looked like a hoary old man.

I was invigorated by honest work and plenty of food during my weeks in Akron, but simply stepping back out onto the highway seemed to draw me back to a lean and hungry look. I felt stooped over, and very, very tired of life on the road. I felt out of practice and at first made only desultory motions to flag down a ride. However, with the cold nipping at my ankles, face, and wrists, I resolved to focus my energies and keep moving. I straightened up, made a smile of my freezing lips, and looked the drivers in the eye as I held out an obvious right thumb from my wool mitten.

Mostly it was local traffic, going a few miles at a time, through the small farm towns of the rolling hills north of Akron. Mostly people just felt sorry for me, the weather being so cold, so they gave me rides even though they weren't going very far. I was grateful for the warmth.

Near Sagamore Hills, I hooked up with another hitchhiker named James, and together we worked our way north, our conversation helping us to not focus on our individual discomfort.

Quite a way south of Cleveland, we were blessed by a good long ride to the north and east, which put us in the town of Mayfield, which was the closest I'd been to home in many years. As we stood beside the road, alternately clapping our hands together or holding them under our arms, we were a bit startled when a big sedan began pulling to the side *before* getting to us. I was a bit nervous, as this was a very unusual occurrence, but the driver waved avidly for us to come to the car. We hustled our gear down to the car and gratefully climbed into the warm auto.

There were a few moments of shuffling bags in and getting ourselves in the car, all the while the driver shouting at us. I had no idea what he was saying until I finally piled into the front seat. When I turned to him to discuss his destination, I was struck silent by the sight of the driver: my brother Bob! He was grinning ear-to-ear, and his eyes glistened. He had seen us as he was driving south and, despite the passing of the years, recognized me from across the road; so he'd turned around to pick us up. Bob and I gave strangled howls and awkwardly attempted a hug in the front seat. Reunited at long last.

After much back-pounding and shouting, we finally settled down enough that Bob put the car in gear, and I spent some time explaining things to James. Bob, having found a lucrative job, soon had us eating food in a little diner, with him and me catching up on how we were doing, status of the family, and so on.

With a full, warm belly, James got out at the crossroad heading toward Erie, and Bob (although he lived in another town) took me to our parents' home. Wisely, he asked me to wait in the car for a few minutes, so as not to give Mother a heart attack, while he went inside. Soon I walked through the old house to where my mother sat, working with the plants that sat perpetually in the south-facing window. She stared up at me a long while, her eyes blinking without comprehension. It was quiet there in the kitchen for a moment, and I became painfully aware of my animal smell, my unkempt appearance, and how I'd aged since seeing my mother. At last, her eyes seemed to focus, and she simply said, "Eddie?" and I bent forward to kiss and hug her, despite my appearance and aroma.

I sat down with Mom and helped her repot a couple of plants. Indeed, I could feel my own roots grasping soil in a new way. The pleasure I felt with my fingers in the black Ohio potting soil was entirely out of proportion with the little job we were doing. "Here it is," I kept repeating to myself... "Here it is." And I haven't wandered far from Mother's garden since that day.

I was returned to the warm embrace of my parents and the two siblings who were still living at home at the time. The Prodigal Son had returned, my journey ended, my independent spirit exhausted. Like those tanker trucks back in Colorado, I was ready to be connected, to help or be helped, and (dare I say it?) to love.

Epilogue

From an Interview in 2011

"Well, that's pretty much my story. Pretty much the way it happened. I'm living a new life now, far different from the one I experienced on my own out in the world.

"You can guess that I really did settle into that spiritual program that I talked about there at the end... it saved my life! I was most miserable and alone, right when I thought I was going to discover the Big Secret of Life, on the West Coast, or in Las Vegas, or in Denver. And here I found love and sanity and companionship back at home!

"I met and married a wonderful girl, the second 'Marie' in my life, and although it hasn't always been easy, we've managed to stay together for many years now. I've remained friends with Francis 'Harley' these many years, as well, and like I said, that boy is a lifesaver. I got a decent job, put a couple of kids through school, and all-in-all my life has gone real well.

"Marie woke me up this morning about six-thirty, with a gentle touch to my knee to wake me slowly. In the split second before I opened my eyes, I already had her wrist in a steel grip. So, some of that 'alone and on the road' stuff is still with me.

"I'm in frequent contact with St. Francis of Akron, and I even exchange Christmas cards with that rascal Michael, who has continued to reside in San Francisco, still, in his own peculiar way, living a counter-cultural life.

"Although I've changed a lot, some basic things about me never have changed. Marie will catch me at some unthinking moment and point out that I'm still my mother's son: feet planted, spine straining, head forward, with my arm pointing straight out in front, still gabbling away, 'Look at that! Now that!'

"I wanna be sure that I don't leave you with the wrong impression. I'm still a vain, opinionated, profane man, but what I've learned since my time on the road is how to *deal* with my shortcomings. I still get broody and give Marie the silent treatment, but now it lasts for hours instead of days. I still meet with those loud, blasphemous, sinners who have been showing me the way these many years since I left off my wandering, and I'm all the better for it. I've found a way that leaves me, and better yet all the people 'round me, happy, and I mean just about every day!

"I helped to attend to Mother and Dad in their final days, and we reconciled long before they died. It's so good to have come full circle in this journey of mine. All is healed here at the end of the road; and I hope my story has some meaning for you."

About the Author

Tim Hoopingarner, PhD, a consultant specializing in Safety Culture Leadership, lives in Bailey, Colorado, with his spouse and two daughters. In his estimate, he has hitchhiked around 50,000 miles.